Jordan moved quickly through the gravestones until he found the one stone that was newer than the others, only six years in the ground.

The name on the tombstone read Mary Justice Cardwell.

"Hello, Mother," he said removing his hat as he felt all the conflicting emotions he'd had when she was alive. All the arguments came rushing back, making him sick at the memory. He hadn't been able to change her mind, and now she was gone, leaving them all behind to struggle as a family without her.

He could almost hear their last argument whispered on the wind. "There is nothing keeping you here, let alone me," he'd argued. "Why are you fighting so hard to keep this place going? Can't you see that ranching is going to kill you?"

He recalled her smile, that gentle gleam in her eyes that infuriated him. "This land is what makes me happy, son. Someday you will realize that ranching is in our blood. You can fight it, but this isn't just your home, a part of your heart is here as well."

"Like hell," he'd said. "Sell the ranch, Mother, before it's too late. If not for yourself and the rest of us, then for Dana. She's too much like you. She will spend her life fighting to keep this place. Don't do that to her."

"She'll keep this ranch for the day when you come back to help her run it."

"That's never going to happen, Mother."

Mary Justice Cardwell had smiled that knowing smile of hers. "Only time will tell, won't it?"

Dear Reader,

It was so much fun for me to return to Cardwell Ranch. *Crime Scene at Cardwell Ranch* has been read by more than two million readers, so it was a treat to go back and find out what happened to the Justice and Cardwell families in the sequel. *Justice at Cardwell Ranch* is a story I've wanted to write for a long time.

When I was a girl, we had a cabin just down the road from where these books take place. I have such wonderful memories of the Gallatin Canyon. My brother and I had a fort out in the woods and spent hours exploring in what is now a wilderness area. I skied at Big Sky many times, and have hiked with a friend to Ousel Waterfalls, where part of this story takes place.

I hope you enjoy this return trip to the "canyon."

B.J. Daniels

www.bjdaniels.com

USA TODAY Bestselling Author

B.J. DANIELS

JUSTICE AT CARDWELL RANCH

HARLEQUIN®

entertain, enrich, inspire™

This book is dedicated to my amazing husband. He makes all this possible along with inspiring me each and every day. Thank you, Parker. Without your love, I couldn't do this.

ISBN-13: 978-0-373-69644-4

JUSTICE AT CARDWELL RANCH

Copyright © 2012 by Barbara Heinlein

Recycling programs for this product may not exist in your area.

ABOUT THE AUTHOR

USA TODAY bestselling author B.J. Daniels wrote her first book after a career as an award-winning newspaper journalist and author of thirty-seven published short stories. That first book, *Odd Man Out*, received a four-and-a-half-star review from *RT Book Reviews* and went on to be nominated for Best Intrigue that year. Since then, she has won numerous awards, including a career achievement award for romantic suspense and many nominations and awards for best book.

Daniels lives in Montana with her husband, Parker, and two springer spaniels, Spot and Jem. When she isn't writing, she snowboards, camps, boats and plays tennis. Daniels is a member of Mystery Writers of America, Sisters in Crime, International Thriller Writers, Kiss of Death and Romance Writers of America.

To contact her, write to B.J. Daniels, P.O. Box 1173, Malta, MT 59538, or email her at bjdaniels@mtintouch.net. Check out her website, www.bjdaniels.com.

Books by B.J. Daniels

HARLEQUIN INTRIGUE

Other titles by this author available in ebook format.

CAST OF CHARACTERS

Jordan Cardwell—The former cowboy bad boy is back in the canyon chasing a secret that would shock the Big Sky community.

Liza Turner—The Deputy Marshal knows Jordan is dangerous. But she's hoping he isn't a murderer.

Dana Cardwell Savage—Pregnant with twins and on doctor prescribed bed rest, all she needs is trouble from her estranged siblings.

Hud Savage—The marshal has his hands full with a pregnant wife and two young children. He doesn't need a murder or two—and a possible kidnapping.

Stacy Cardwell—She left the canyon six years ago, but now she is back with a surprise package and trouble at her heels.

Clay Cardwell—He has his reasons for disappearing six months ago.

Tanner Cole—He learned the hard way about a woman scorned.

Shelby Durran-Iverson—She has a way of getting what she wants. But if her secret comes out, no one will be able to help her, not even her closest friends.

Alex Winslow—He thinks he's found a way to even a few scores and make his bad life better.

Tessa Ryerson Spring—She has a lot of reasons to be resentful of her best friend.

Prologue

Nothing moved in the darkness. At the corner of the house she stopped to catch her breath. She could hear music playing somewhere down the street. Closer, a dog barked.

As she waited in the deep shadow at the edge of the house, she measured the distance and the light she would have to pass through to reach the second window.

When she'd sneaked into the house earlier, she'd left the window unlocked. But she had no way of knowing if someone had discovered it. If so, they might not have merely relocked it—they could be waiting for her.

Fear had her heart pounding and her breath coming out in painful bursts. If she got caught— She couldn't let herself think about that.

The dog stopped barking for a moment. All she could hear was the faint music drifting on the night breeze. She fought to keep her breathing in check as she inched along the side of the house to the first window.

A light burned inside, but the drapes were closed. Still, she waited to make sure she couldn't hear anyone on the other side of the glass before she moved.

Ducking, she slipped quickly through a shaft of illumination from a streetlamp and stopped at the second bedroom window.

There, she waited for a few moments. No light burned inside the room. Still she listened before she pulled the screwdriver from her jacket pocket and began to pry up the window.

At first the old casement window didn't move and she feared she'd been right about someone discovering what she'd done and locking the window again.

When it finally gave, it did so with a pop that sounded like an explosion to her ears. She froze. No sound came from within the room. Her hands shook as she pried the window up enough that she could get her fingers under it.

Feeling as if there was no turning back now, she lifted the window enough to climb in. Heart in her throat, she drew back the curtain. She'd half expected to find someone standing on the other side lying in wait for her.

The room, painted pink, was empty except for a few pieces of mismatched furniture: a dresser, a rocking chair, a changing table and a crib.

She looked to the crib, fearing that she'd come this far only to fail. But from the faint light coming from the streetlamp, she could see the small lump beneath the tiny quilt.

Her heart beat faster at the thought that in a few minutes she would have the baby in her arms.

She heard the car coming down the street just seconds before the headlights washed over her. Halfway in the window, there was nothing she could do but hurry. She wasn't leaving here without the baby.

Chapter One

The breeze rustled through the aspens, sending golden leaves whirling around him as Jordan Cardwell walked up the hill to the cemetery. He wore a straw Western hat he'd found on a peg by the back door of the ranch house.

He hadn't worn a cowboy hat since he'd left Montana twenty years ago, but this one kept his face from burning. It was so much easier to get sunburned at this high altitude than it was in New York City.

It was hot out and yet he could feel the promise of winter hiding at the edge of the fall day. Only the memory of summer remained in the Gallatin River Canyon. Cold nightly temperatures had turned the aspens to glittering shades of gold and orange against the dark green of the pines.

Below him he could hear the rushing water of the Gallatin as the river cut a deep winding course through the canyon. Across the river, sheer granite cliffs rose up to where the sun hung in a faded blue big Montana sky.

As he walked, the scent of crushed dry leaves beneath his soles sent up the remembered smell of other autumns. He knew this land. As hard as he'd tried to escape it, this place was branded on him, this life as familiar as his own heartbeat—even after all these years.

He thought of all the winters he'd spent in this canyon listening to the ice crack on the river, feeling the bite of snow as it blew off a pine bough to sting his face, breathing in a bone-deep cold that made his head ache.

He'd done his time here, he thought as he turned his face up to the last of the day's warmth before the sun disappeared behind the cliffs. Soon the aspens would be bare, the limbs dark against a winter-washed pale frosty sky. The water in the horse troughs would begin to freeze and so would the pooling eddies along the edge of the river. The cold air in the shade of the pines was a warning of what was to come, he thought as he reached the wrought-iron cemetery gate.

The gate groaned as he shoved it open. He hesitated. What was he doing here? Nearby the breeze sighed in the tops of the towering pines, drawing his attention to the dense stand. He didn't remember them being so tall. Or so dark and thick. As he watched the boughs sway, he told himself to make this quick. He didn't want to get caught here.

Even though it was a family cemetery, he didn't feel welcome here anymore. His own fault, but still, it could get messy if anyone from his family caught him on the ranch. He didn't plan to stick around long enough to see any of them. It was best that way, he told himself as he stepped through the gate into the small cemetery.

He'd never liked graveyards. Nor did it give him any comfort to know that more than a dozen remains of their relatives were interred here. He took no satisfaction in the long lineage of the Justice family, let alone the Cardwell one, in this canyon—unlike his sister.

Dana found strength in knowing that their ancestors had been mule-headed ranchers who'd weathered everything Montana had thrown at them to stay on this ranch. They'd settled this land along a stretch of the Gallatin, a crystal clear trout stream that ran over a hundred miles from Yellowstone Park to the Missouri River.

The narrow canyon got little sunlight each day. In the winter it was an icebox of frost and snow. Getting up to feed the animals had been pure hell. He'd never understood why any of them had stayed.

But they had, he thought as he surveyed the tombstones. They'd fought this land to remain here and now they would spend eternity in soil that had given them little in return for their labors.

A gust of wind rattled through the colorful aspen leaves and moaned in the high branches of the pines. Dead foliage floated like gold coins around him, showering the weather-bleached gravestones. He was reminded why he'd never liked coming up to this wind-blown hill. He found no peace among the dead. Nor had he come here today looking for it.

He moved quickly through the gravestones until he found the one stone that was newer than the others, only six years in the ground. The name on the tombstone read Mary Justice Cardwell.

"Hello, Mother," he said removing his hat as he felt all the conflicting emotions he'd had when she was alive. All the arguments came rushing back, making him sick at the memory. He hadn't been able to change her mind and now she was gone, leaving them all behind to struggle as a family without her.

He could almost hear their last argument whispered on the wind. "There is nothing keeping you here, let alone me," he'd argued. "Why are you fighting so hard to keep this place going? Can't you see that ranching is going to kill you?"

He recalled her smile, that gentle gleam in her eyes that infuriated him. "This land is what makes me happy, son. Someday you will realize that ranching is in our blood. You can fight it, but this isn't just your home. A part of your heart is here, as well."

"Like hell," he'd said. "Sell the ranch, Mother, before it's too late. If not for yourself and the rest of us, then for Dana. She's too much like you. She will spend her life fighting to keep this place. Don't do that to her."

"She'll keep this ranch for the day when you come back to help her run it."

"That's never going to happen, Mother."

Mary Justice Cardwell had smiled that knowing smile of hers. "Only time will tell, won't it?"

Jordan turned the hat brim nervously in his fingers as he looked down at his mother's grave and searched for the words to tell her how much he hated what she'd done to him. To all of them. But to his surprise he felt tears well in his eyes, his throat constricting on a gulf of emotion he hadn't anticipated.

A gust of wind bent the pine boughs and blew down to scatter dried leaves across the landscape. His skin rippled with goosebumps as he suddenly sensed someone watching him. His head came up, his gaze going to the darkness of the pines.

She was only a few yards away. He hadn't heard the woman on horseback approach and realized she must have been there the whole time, watching him.

She sat astride a large buckskin horse. Shadows played across her face from the swaying pine boughs. The breeze lifted the long dark hair that flowed like molten obsidian over her shoulders and halfway down her back.

There was something vaguely familiar about her. But if he'd known her years before when this was home, he couldn't place her now. He'd been gone too long from Montana.

And yet a memory tugged at him. His gaze settled on her face again, the wide-set green eyes, that piercing look that seemed to cut right to his soul.

With a curse, he knew where he'd seen her before—and why she was looking at him the way she was. A shudder moved through him as if someone had just walked over *his* grave.

LIZA TURNER HAD WATCHED the man slog up the hill, his footsteps slow, his head down, as if he were going to a funeral. So she hadn't been surprised when he'd pushed open the gate to the cemetery and stepped in.

At first, after reining her horse in under the pines, she'd been mildly curious. She loved this spot, loved looking across the canyon as she rode through the groves of aspens and pines. It was always cool in the trees. She liked listening to the river flowing emerald-green below her on the hillside and taking a moment to search the granite cliffs on the other side for mountain sheep.

She hadn't expected to see anyone on her ride this morning. When she'd driven into the ranch for her usual trek, she'd seen the Cardwell Ranch pickup leaving and remembered that Hud was taking Dana into Bozeman today for her doctor's appointment. They were leaving the kids with Dana's best friend and former business partner, Hilde at Needles and Pins, the local fabric store.

The only other person on the ranch was the aging ranch manager, Warren Fitzpatrick. Warren would be watching *Let's Make a Deal* at his cabin this time of the morning.

So Liza had been curious and a bit leery when she'd first laid eyes on the stranger in the Western straw hat. As far as she knew, no one else should have been on the ranch today. So who was this tall, broad-shouldered cowboy?

Dana had often talked about hiring some help since Warren was getting up in years and she had her hands full with a four- and five-year-old, not to mention now being pregnant with twins.

But if this man was the new hired hand, why would he be interested in the Justice-Cardwell family cemetery? She felt the skin on the back of her neck prickle. There was something about this cowboy... His face had been in shadow from the brim of his hat. When he'd stopped at one of the graves and had taken his hat off, head bowed, she still hadn't been able to see more than his profile from where she sat astride her horse.

Shifting in the saddle, she'd tried to get a better look. He must have heard the creak of leather or sensed her presence. His head came up, his gaze darting right to the spot where she sat. He looked startled at first, then confused as if he was trying to place her.

She blinked, not sure she could trust her eyes. *Jordan Cardwell?*

He looked completely different from the arrogant man in the expensive three-piece suit she'd crossed paths with six years ago. He wore jeans, a button-up shirt and work boots. He looked tanned and stronger as if he'd been doing manual labor. There was only a hint of the earlier arrogance in his expression, making him more handsome than she remembered.

She saw the exact moment when he recognized her. Bitterness burned in his dark gaze as a small resentful smile tugged at his lips.

Oh, yes, it was Jordan Cardwell all right, she thought, wondering what had made her think he was handsome just moments before or—even harder to believe, that he might have changed.

Six years ago he'd been the number one suspect in a murder as well as a suspect in an attempted murder. Liza had been the deputy who'd taken his fingerprints.

She wondered now what he was doing not only back in the canyon, but also on the ranch he and his siblings had fought so hard to take from their sister Dana.

DANA SAVAGE LAY BACK ON THE examining table, nervously picking at a fingernail. "I can't remember the last time I saw my feet," she said with a groan.

Dr. Pamela Burr laughed. "This might feel a little cold."

Dana tried not to flinch as the doctor applied clear jelly to her huge stomach. She closed her eyes and waited until she heard the heartbeats before she opened them again. "So everything is okay?"

"Your babies appear to be doing fine. Don't you want to look?"

Dana didn't look at the monitor. "You know Hud. He's determined to be surprised. Just like the last two. So I don't dare look." She shot a glance at her husband. He stood next to her, his gaze on her, not the screen. He smiled, but she could see he was worried.

The doctor shut off the machine. "As for the spotting…"

Dana felt her heart drop as she saw the concern in Dr. Burr's expression.

"I'm going to have to insist on bed rest for these last weeks," she said. "Let's give these babies the best start we can by leaving them where they are for now." She looked to Hud.

"You can count on me," he said. "It's Dana you need to convince."

Dana sat up and laid her hands over her extended stomach. She felt the twins moving around in the cramped space. Poor babies. "Okay."

"You understand what bed rest means?" the doctor asked. "No ranch business, no getting up except to shower and use the bathroom. You're going to need help with Hank and Mary."

That was putting it mildly when you had a four- and five-year-old who were wild as the canyon where they lived.

"I'm sure Hud—"

"You'll need more than his help." The doctor pressed a piece of paper into her hand. "These are several women you might call that I've used before."

Dana didn't like the idea of bringing in a stranger to take care of Hud and the kids, but the babies kicked and she nodded.

"Doc said I was going to have to watch you like a hawk," Hud told her on the way home. Apparently while she was getting dressed, Dr. Burr had been bending his ear, down the hall in her office. "You always try to do too much. With the kids, the ranch, me—"

"I'll be good."

He gave her a disbelieving look.

"Marshal, would you like a sworn affidavit?"

He grinned over at her. "Actually, I'm thinking about handcuffing you to the bed. I reckon it will be the only way I can keep you down for a day let alone weeks."

Dana groaned as she realized how hard it was going to be to stay in bed. "What about Hank and Mary? They won't understand why their mommy can't be up and around, let alone outside with them and their animals." Both of them had their own horses and loved to ride.

"I've already put in for a leave. Liza can handle things. Anyway, it's in between resort seasons so it's quiet."

September through the middle of November was slow around Big Sky with the summer tourists gone and ski season still at least a month away.

Dana knew October was probably a better time than any other for her husband to be off work. That wasn't the problem. "Hud, I hate to see you have to babysit me and the kids."

"It's not babysitting when it's *your* wife and kids, Dana."

"You know what I mean. There are the kids and the ranch—"

"Honey, you've been trying to do it all for too long."

She *had* been juggling a lot of balls for some time now, but Hud always helped on the weekends. Their ranch manager, Warren Fitzpatrick, was getting up in years so he had really slowed down. But Warren was a fixture around the ranch, one she couldn't afford to replace. More than anything, she loved the hands-on part of ranching so she spent as much time as she could working the land.

When she'd found out she was pregnant this time she'd been delighted, but a little worried how she was going to handle another child right now.

Then the doctor had told her she was having twins. *Twins?* Seriously?

"Are you all right?" Hud asked as he placed his hand over hers and squeezed.

She smiled and nodded. "I'm always all right when I'm with you."

He gave her hand another squeeze before he went back to driving. "I'm taking you home. Then I'll go by the shop and pick up the kids." Her friend Hilde had the kids in Big Sky. "But I'd better not find out you were up and about while I was gone."

Dana shook her head and made a cross with her finger over her heart. She lay back and closed her eyes, praying as she had since the spotting had begun that the babies she was carrying would be all right. Mary and Hank were so excited about the prospect of two little brothers or sisters. She couldn't disappoint them.

She couldn't disappoint anyone, especially her mother, she thought. While Mary Justice Cardwell had been gone six years now, she was as much a part of the ranch as the old, two-story house where Dana lived with Hud and the kids. Her mother had trusted her to keep Cardwell Ranch going. Against all odds she was doing her darnedest to keep that promise.

So why did she feel so scared, as if waiting for the other shoe to drop?

Chapter Two

Jordan watched Deputy Liza Turner ride her horse out of the pines. The past six years had been good to her. She'd been pretty back then. Now there was a confidence as if she'd grown into the woman she was supposed to become. He recalled how self-assured and efficient she'd been at her job. She was also clearly at home on the back of a horse.

The trees cast long shadows over the stark landscape. Wind whirled the dried leaves that now floated in the air like snowflakes.

"Jordan Cardwell," she said as she reined in her horse at the edge of the cemetery.

He came out through the gate, stopping to look up at her. "Deputy." She had one of those faces that was almost startling in its uniqueness. The green eyes wide, captivating and always filled with curiosity. He thought she was more interesting than he remembered. That, he realized, was probably because she was out of uniform.

She wore jeans and a red-checked Western shirt that made her dark hair appear as rich as mahogany. She narrowed those green eyes at him. Curiosity and suspicion, he thought.

"I'm surprised to see you here," she said, a soft lilt

to her voice. She had a small gap between her two front teeth, an imperfection, that he found charming.

"I don't know why you'd be surprised. My sister might have inherited the ranch but I'm still family."

She smiled at that and he figured she knew all about what had happened after his mother had died—and her new will had gone missing.

"I didn't think you'd ever come back to the ranch," she said.

He chuckled. "Neither did I. But people change."

"Do they?" She was studying him in a way that said she doubted he had. He didn't need to read her expression to know she was also wondering what kind of trouble he'd brought back to the canyon with him. The horse moved under her, no doubt anxious to get going.

"Your horse seems impatient," he said. "Don't let me keep you from your ride." With a tip of his hat, he headed down the mountain to the ranch house where he'd been raised.

It seemed a lifetime ago. He could barely remember the man he'd been then. But he would be glad to get off the property before his sister and her husband returned. He planned to put off seeing them if at all possible. So much for family, he thought.

WHEN DANA OPENED HER EYES, she saw that they'd left the wide valley and were now driving through the Gallatin Canyon. The "canyon" as it was known, ran from the mouth just south of Gallatin Gateway almost to West Yellowstone, fifty miles of winding road that trailed the river in a deep cut through the mountains.

The drive along the Gallatin River had always been breathtaking, a winding strip of highway that followed the blue-ribbon trout stream up over the continental divide. This time of year the Gallatin ran crystal clear over green-tinted boulders. Pine trees grew dark and thick along its edge and against the steep mountains. Aspens, their leaves rust-reds and glittering golds, grew among the pines.

Sheer rock cliffs overlooked the highway and river, with small areas of open land, the canyon not opening up until it reached Big Sky. The canyon had been mostly cattle and dude ranches, a few summer cabins and homes—that was until Big Sky resort and the small town that followed at the foot of Lone Mountain.

Luxury houses had sprouted up all around the resort. Fortunately, some of the original cabins still remained and the majority of the canyon was national forest so it would always remain undeveloped. The "canyon" was also still its own little community, for which Dana was grateful. This was the only home she'd known and, like her stubborn ancestors, she had no intention of ever leaving it.

Both she and Hud had grown up here. They'd been in love since junior high, but hit a rocky spot some years ago thanks to her sister. Dana didn't like to think about the five years she and Hud had spent apart as they passed the lower mountain resort area and, a few miles farther, turned down the road to Cardwell Ranch.

Across the river and a half mile back up a wide valley, the Cardwell Ranch house sat against a backdrop of granite cliffs, towering dark pines and glittering aspens. The house was a big, two-story rambling affair with a wide front porch and a brick-red metal roof. Behind it stood a huge weathered barn and some outbuildings and corrals.

Dana never felt truly at home until they reached the ranch she'd fought tooth and nail to save. When Mary Justice Cardwell had been bucked off a horse and died six years ago, Dana had thought all was lost. Her mother's original will when her children were young left the ranch to all of them.

Mary hadn't realized until her children were grown that only Dana would keep the ranch. The others would sell it, take the profits and never look back until the day they regretted what they'd done. By then it would be too late. So her mother had made a new will, leaving the ranch to her. But her mother had hidden it where she hoped her daughter would find it. Fortunately, Dana had found it in time to save the ranch.

The will had put an end to her siblings' struggle to force her to sell the land and split the profits with them. Now her three siblings were paid part of the ranch's profit each quarter. Not surprisingly, she hadn't heard from any of them since the will had settled things six years before.

As Hud pulled into the ranch yard, Dana spotted a car parked in front of the old house and frowned. The car was an older model with California plates.

"You didn't already hire someone—"

"No," Hud said before she could finish. "I wouldn't do that without talking to you first. Do you think the doctor called one of the women she told you about?"

Before Dana could answer, she saw that someone was waiting out on the broad front porch. As Hud pulled in beside the car, the woman stepped from out of the shadows.

"Stacy?" She felt her heart drop. After six years

of silence and all the bad feelings from the past, what was her older sister doing here?

"SURPRISE," STACY SAID WITH a shrug and a worried smile. Like Dana, Stacy had gotten the Justice-Cardwell dark good looks, but she'd always been the cute one who capitalized on her appearance, cashing in as she traded her way up through three marriages that Dana knew of and possibly more since.

Just the sight of her sister made Dana instantly wary. She couldn't help but be mistrustful given their past.

Her sister's gaze went to Dana's stomach. "Oh, my. You're *pregnant*."

"We need to get Dana in the house," Hud said, giving his sister-in-law a nod of greeting. Stacy opened the door and let them enter before she followed them in.

Dana found herself looking around the living room, uncomfortable that her sister had been inside the house even though it had once been Stacy's home, as well.

The house was as it had been when her mother was alive. Original Western furnishings, a lot of stone and wood and a bright big airy kitchen. Dana, like her mother, chose comfort over style trends. She loved her big, homey house. It often smelled of something good bubbling on the stove, thanks to the fact that Hud loved to cook.

Dana preferred to spend her time with her children outside, teaching them to ride or watching a new foal being born or picking fresh strawberries out of the large garden she grew—just as her own mother had done with her.

As she looked at her sister, she was reminded of some of her mother's last words to her. "Families stick together. It isn't always easy. Everyone makes mistakes. Dana, you have to find forgiveness in your heart. If not for them, then for yourself."

Her mother had known then that if anything happened to her, Jordan, Stacy and Clay would fight her for the ranch. That's why she'd made the new will.

But she must also have known that the will would divide them.

"It's been a long time," Dana said, waiting, knowing her sister wanted something or she wouldn't be here.

"I know I should have kept in touch more," Stacy said. "I move around a lot." But she'd always managed to get her check each quarter as part of her inheritance from the ranch profits. Dana instantly hated the uncharitable thought. She didn't want to feel that way about her sister. But Stacy had done some things in the past that had left the two of them at odds. Like breaking Dana and Hud up eleven years ago. Dana still had trouble forgiving her sister for that.

Stacy shifted uncomfortably in the silence. "I should have let you know I was coming, huh."

"Now isn't the best time for company," Hud said. "Dana's doctor has advised her to get off her feet for the rest of her pregnancy."

"But I'm not *company,*" Stacy said. "I'm family. I can help."

Hud looked to his wife. "Why don't you go. It's fine," Dana said and removed her coat.

"So you're pregnant," her sister said.

"Twins," Dana said, sinking into a chair.

Stacy nodded.

Dana realized Hud was still in his coat, waiting,

afraid to leave her alone with Stacy. "Are you going to pick up the kids?"

He gave her a questioning look.

"I thought you probably had more kids," her sister said. "The toys and stuff around."

Dana was still looking at her husband. She knew he didn't trust Stacy, hated she'd been alone in their house while they were gone and worse, he didn't want to leave the two of them alone. "Stacy and I will be fine."

Still he hesitated. He knew better than anyone what her siblings were like.

"Stacy, would you mind getting me a drink of water?" The moment her sister left the room, Dana turned to her husband. "I'll be *fine,*" she said lowering her voice. "Go pick up the kids. I promise I won't move until you get back." She could tell that wasn't what had him concerned.

He glanced toward the kitchen and the sound of running water. "I won't be long."

She motioned him over and smiled as he leaned down to kiss her. At the same time, he placed a large hand on her swollen stomach. The babies moved and he smiled.

"You have your cell phone if you need me?"

Dana nodded. "The marshal's office is also on speed dial. I'll be fine. Really."

Stacy came back in with a glass full of water as Hud left. "I'm glad things have turned out good for you. Hud is so protective."

"Thank you," she said as she took the glass and studied her sister over the rim as she took a drink.

"I would have called," Stacy said, "but I wanted to surprise you."

"I'm surprised." She watched her sister move

around the room, touching one object after another, seeming nervous. Her first thought when she'd seen her sister was that she'd come here because she was in trouble.

That initial observation hadn't changed. Now though, Dana was betting it had something to do with money. It usually did with Stacy, unfortunately.

Years ago Dana had found out just how low her sister would stoop if the price was right. She had good reason not to trust her sister.

"The place hasn't changed at all," Stacy was saying now. "Except for the pile of toys in the sunroom. I heard Hud say he was going to pick up the kids?"

"Hank and Mary, five and four."

"You named your daughter after mother, that's nice," Stacy said. "I thought you probably would." She seemed to hear what she'd said. "I want you to know I'm not upset about mother leaving you the ranch. You know me, I would have just blown the money." She flashed a self-deprecating smile. "And you're pregnant with twins! When are you due?"

"Eight weeks." When she finally couldn't take it anymore, Dana asked, "Stacy, what are you doing here?"

"It's kind of a strange story," her sister said, looking even more nervous.

Dana braced herself. If Stacy thought it was a strange story, then it could be anything. Her sister opened her mouth to say something, but was interrupted.

From upstairs a baby began to cry.

"What is that?" Dana demanded.

"I haven't had a chance to tell you," Stacy said as she started for the stairs. "That's Ella. That's my other surprise. I have a baby."

LIZA PARKED HER PICKUP ACROSS the road from Trail's End and settled in to wait. She had a clear view of the small cabin Jordan had rented. Like a lot of Big Sky, the string of cabins were new. But it being off-season and the cabins' only view being Highway 191, she figured they weren't too pricey. She wondered how Jordan was fixed for money and if that's what had brought him back here.

Pulling out her phone, she called Hud's cell. He answered on the third ring. She could hear the kids in the background and a woman's voice. Hilde, Dana's best friend. He must be at Needles and Pins.

"How's Dana, boss?" she asked.

"Stubborn."

She laughed. "So the doctor *did* prescribe bed rest."

"Yes. Fortunately, I know you can run things just fine without me."

"Probably more smoothly without you around," she joked.

He must have heard something in her voice. "But?"

"Nothing I can't handle," she assured him. "But you might want to give Dana a heads-up."

"Dana already knows. Stacy's at the house right now."

"Stacy?"

"Who were *you* talking about?" Hud asked.

"Jordan."

She heard Hud swear under his breath.

"I saw him earlier on the ranch, actually at the family cemetery," Liza said.

"What's he doing in the canyon?"

"He didn't say, but I found out where he's staying. He's rented a cabin past Buck's T-4." Buck's T-4 was a local landmark bar and hotel. "I'm hanging out, watching to see what he's up to."

"Probably not the best way to spend taxpayers' dollars, but I appreciate it. As far as I know, he hasn't contacted Dana."

"Let me know if he does. In the meantime, I'll stick around here for a while."

"You really need to get a life, deputy," Hud said. "Thanks. Let me know if you need help."

"So Stacy's here, too?"

"We haven't heard from any of them in six years and now two of them are in the canyon? This doesn't bode well."

That had been her thought exactly.

"I don't want them upsetting Dana," he said. "All we need is for Clay to show up next. This couldn't come at a worse time. I'm worried enough about Dana and the babies. I have a bad feeling this could have something to do with that developer who's been after Dana to sell some of the ranch."

"The timing does make you wonder," Liza said.

"I'm going back to the ranch now."

"You stick close to Dana. I'll let you know if Jordan heads for the ranch." Hanging up, Liza settled in again. She knew it could be a while. Jordan might be in for the night.

The canyon got dark quickly this time of year. With the dark that settled over it like a cloak came a drop in temperature. She could hear the river, smell the rich scent of fall. A breeze stirred the nearby pines, making the branches sway and sigh. A couple of stars popped out above the canyon walls.

The door of the cabin opened. Jordan stepped out

and headed for his rented SUV parked outside. He was dressed in a warm coat, gloves and a hat, all in a dark color. He definitely didn't look like a man going out for dinner—or even to visit his sister. He glanced around as if he thought someone might be watching him before climbing into his rental.

Liza felt her heart kick up a beat as she slunk down in the pickup seat and waited. A few moments later she heard the SUV pull out. She started the truck, and sitting up, followed at a distance.

To her relief, he didn't turn down Highway 191 in the direction of the Cardwell Ranch—and his sister's house. Instead, he headed north toward Big Sky proper, making her think she might be wrong. Maybe he was merely going out to find a place to have dinner.

He drove on past the lighted buildings that made up the Meadow Village, heading west toward Mountain Village. There was little traffic this time of year. She let another vehicle get between them, all the time keeping Jordan's taillights in sight.

Just when she started speculating on where he might be headed, he turned off on the road to Ousel Falls. They passed a few commercial buildings, a small housing complex and then the road cut through the pines as it climbed toward the falls.

Liza pulled over, letting him get farther ahead. Had he spotted the tail? She waited as long as she dared before she drove on up the road. Her headlights cut a gold swath through the darkness. Dense pines lined both sides of the mountain road. There was no traffic at all up this way. She worried he had spotted her following him and was now leading her on a wild-goose chase.

She hadn't gone far when her headlights picked up

the parking lot for the falls. Jordan's rental was parked in the empty lot. She couldn't tell if he was still in the vehicle. Grabbing her baseball cap off the seat, she covered her dark hair as she drove on past.

Out of the corner of her eye she saw that the SUV was empty. Past it near the trailhead, she glimpsed the beam of a flashlight bobbing as it headed down the trail.

A few hundred yards up the road Liza found a place to pull over. She grabbed her own flashlight from under the seat, checked to make sure the batteries were still working and got out of the truck.

It was a short hike back to the trailhead. From there the path dropped to the creek before rising again as it twisted its way through the thick forest.

The trail was wide and paved and she found, once her eyes adjusted, that she didn't need to use her flashlight if she was careful. Enough starlight bled down through the pine boughs that she could see far enough ahead—and she knew the trail well.

There was no sign of Jordan, though. She'd reached the creek and bridge, quickly crossed it, and had started up the winding track when she caught a glimpse of light above her on the footpath.

She stopped to listen, afraid he might have heard her behind him. But there was only the sound of the creek and moan of the pines in the breeze. Somewhere in the distance an owl hooted. She moved again, hurrying now.

Once the pathway topped out, she should be able to see Jordan's light ahead of her, though she couldn't imagine what he was doing hiking to the falls tonight.

There was always a good chance of running into a

moose or a wolf or worse this time of a year, a hungry grizzly foraging for food before hibernation.

The trail topped out. She stopped to catch her breath and listen for Jordan. Ahead she could make out the solid rock area at the base of the waterfall. A few more steps and she could feel the mist coming off the cascading water. From here, the walkway carved a crooked path up through the pines to the top of the falls.

There was no sign of any light ahead and the only thing she could hear was rushing water. Where was Jordan? She moved on, convinced he was still ahead of her. Something rustled in the trees off to her right. A limb cracked somewhere ahead in the pines.

She stopped and drew her weapon. Someone was out there.

The report of the rifle shot felt so close it made the hair stand up on her neck. The sound ricocheted off the rock cliff and reverberated through her. Liza dove to the ground. A second shot echoed through the trees.

Weapon drawn, she scrambled up the hill and almost tripped over the body Jordan Cardwell was standing over.

Chapter Three

"You have a *baby*?" Dana said, still shocked when Stacy came back downstairs carrying a pink bundle. "I'm just having a hard time imagining you as a mother."

"You think you're the only one with a maternal instinct?" Stacy sounded hurt.

"I guess I never thought you *wanted* a baby."

Stacy gave a little shrug. "People change."

Did they? Dana wondered as she studied her sister.

"Want to see her?" Stacy asked.

Dana nodded and her sister carefully transferred the bundle into her arms. Dana saw that it wasn't a blanket at all that the baby was wrapped in, but a cute pink quilt. Parting the edges, she peered in at the baby. A green-eyed knockout stared back at her.

"Isn't she *beautiful*?"

"She's breathtaking. What's her name?"

"Ella."

Dana looked up at her sister, her gaze going to Stacy's bare left-hand ring finger. "Is there a father?"

"Of course," her sister said with an embarrassed laugh. "He's in the military. We're getting married when he comes home in a few weeks."

Stacy had gone through men like tissues during a sad

movie. In the past she'd married for money. Maybe this time she had found something more important, Dana hoped, glancing down at the baby in her arms.

"Hello, Ella," she said to the baby. The bow-shaped lips turned up at the corners, the green eyes sparkling. "How old is she?"

"Six months."

As the baby began to fuss, Stacy dug in a diaper bag Dana hadn't seen at the end of the couch. She pulled out a bottle before going into the kitchen to warm it.

Dana stared at the precious baby, her heart in her throat. She couldn't imagine her sister with a baby. In the past Stacy couldn't even keep a houseplant alive.

As her sister came out of the kitchen, Dana started to hand back the baby.

"You can feed her if you want."

Dana took the bottle and watched the baby suck enthusiastically at the warm formula. "She's adorable." Her sister didn't seem to be listening though.

Stacy had walked over to the window and was looking out. "I forgot how quiet it is here." She hugged herself as a gust of wind rattled the old window. "Or how cold it is this time of year."

"Where *have* you been living?"

"Southern California," she said, turning away from the window.

"Is that where you met the father?"

Stacy nodded. "It's getting late. Ella and I should go."

"Where are you *going?*" Dana asked, alarmed, realizing that she'd been cross-examining her sister as if Stacy was one of Hud's suspects. She couldn't bear the thought of this baby being loaded into that old car outside with Stacy at the wheel.

"I planned to get a motel for the night. Kurt's got some relatives up by Great Falls. They've offered me a place to stay until he gets leave and we can find a place of our own."

Dana shook her head, still holding tight to the baby. "You're staying here. You and Ella can have Mary's room. I don't want you driving at night."

LIZA SWUNG THE BARREL OF HER gun and snapped on her flashlight, aiming both at Jordan. "Put your hands up," she ordered.

He didn't move. He stood stock-still, staring down at the body at his feet. He appeared to be in shock.

"I said put your hands up," she ordered again. He blinked and slowly raised his gaze to her, then lifted his hands. Keeping the gun trained on him, she quickly frisked him. "Where is the weapon?" She nudged him with the point of her gun barrel.

He shook his head. "*I* didn't shoot him."

Liza took a step back from him and shone the flashlight beam into the pines. The light didn't go far in the dense trees and darkness. "Who shot him?"

"I don't know."

She squatted down to check for a pulse. None. Pulling out her phone, she called for backup and the coroner. When she'd finished, she turned the beam on Jordan again. "You can start by telling me what you're doing out here."

He looked down at the body, then up at her. "You know I didn't kill him."

"How do I know that?"

True, she hadn't seen him carrying a rifle, but he could have hidden one in the woods earlier today. But how did he get rid of it so quickly? She would have heard him throw it into the trees.

"What are you doing here at the falls in the middle of the night?"

He looked away.

She began to read him his rights.

"All right," he said with a sigh. "You aren't going to believe me. I was meeting him here."

"To buy drugs?"

"No." He looked insulted. "It's a long story."

"We seem to have time." She motioned to a downed tree not far from the body but deep enough in the trees that if the killer was still out there, he wouldn't have a clear shot.

Jordan sighed as he sat down, dropping his head in his hands for a few moments. "When I was in high school my best friend hung himself. At least that's what everyone thought, anyway. I didn't believe he would do that, but there was no evidence of foul play. Actually, no one believed me when I argued there was no way Tanner would have taken his own life."

"People often say that about suicide victims."

"Yeah. Well, a few weeks ago, I got a call from…" He looked in the direction of the body, but quickly turned away. "Alex Winslow."

"Is that the victim?"

He nodded. "Alex asked if I was coming back for our twenty-year high-school reunion."

"You *were?*" She couldn't help her surprise.

He gave her an are-you-kidding look. "I told him no. That's when he mentioned Tanner."

"Alex Winslow told you he was looking into Tanner's death?"

"Not in so many words. He said something like, 'Do you ever think about Tanner?' He sounded like he'd been drinking. At first I just thought it was the booze talking."

He told her about the rest of the conversation, apparently quoting Alex as best as he could remember.

"Man, it would take something to hang yourself," Alex had said. "Put that noose around your neck and stand there balancing on nothing more than a log stump. One little move... Who would do that unless they were forced to? You know, like at gunpoint or...I don't know, maybe get tricked into standing up there?"

"What are you saying?"

"Just...what if he didn't do it? What if they killed him?"

"They? Who?"

"Don't listen to me. I've had a few too many beers tonight. So, are you sure I can't talk you into coming to the reunion? Even if I told you I have a theory about Tanner's death."

"What theory?"

"Come to the reunion. Call me when you get into town and I'll tell you. Don't mention this to anyone else. Seriously. I don't want to end up like poor old Tanner."

"That could have just been the alcohol talking," Liza said when he finished.

"That's what I thought, too, until he wanted to meet at the falls after dark. Something had him running scared."

"With good reason, apparently. Alex Winslow is a former friend?"

Jordan nodded.

"You weren't just a little suspicious, meeting in the dark at a waterfall?"

"I thought he was being paranoid, but I played along."

"You didn't consider it might be dangerous?"

"No, I thought Alex was overreacting. He was like that. Or at least he had been in high school. I haven't seen him in twenty years."

"Why, if he knew something, did he wait all these years?"

Jordan shrugged. "I just know that Tanner wouldn't have killed himself. He was a smart guy. If anything he was too smart for his own good. I figured if there was even a small chance that Alex knew something…" He glanced over at her. "Apparently, Alex had reason to be paranoid. This proves that there is more to Tanner's suicide."

She heard the determination in his voice and groaned inwardly. "This proves nothing except that Alex Winslow is dead." But Jordan wasn't listening.

"Also it proves I wasn't such a fool to believe Alex really did know something about Tanner's death."

She studied Jordan for a moment. "Did he say something to you before he was shot?"

His gaze shifted away. "I can't even be sure I heard him right."

"What did he say?"

"Shelby."

"Shelby?"

He nodded. "We went to school with a girl named Shelby Durran. She and Tanner were a couple. At least until Christmas our senior year."

HUD HAD JUST RETURNED with the kids when he got the call about the shooting.

"Go," Dana said. "I'll be fine. Stacy is here. She said she'd have the kids help her make dinner for all of us."

He mugged a face and lowered his voice. "Your sister *cooking?* Now that's frightening."

"Go," his wife ordered, giving him a warning look. "We can manage without you for a while."

"Are you sure?" He took her hand and squeezed it. "You promise to stay right where you are?"

"Promise."

Still, he hesitated. He'd been shocked to walk into the house and see Dana holding a baby. For a few moments, he'd been confused as to where she'd gotten it.

"Has Stacy said anything about where she's been?" he asked, glancing toward the kitchen. He could hear the voices of his children and sister-in-law. They all sounded excited about whatever they were making for dinner.

"Southern California. She's headed for Great Falls. There's a military base located there so that makes sense since she says the baby's father is in the military."

"If Stacy can be believed," he said quietly.

Dana mugged a face at him. But telling the truth wasn't one of her sister's strong suits. It bothered him that Dana was defending her sister. He figured the baby had something to do with it. Dana was a sucker for kids.

"Stacy seems different now," she said. "I think it's the baby. It seems to have grounded her some, maybe."

"Maybe," he said doubtfully.

"Go on, you have a murder investigation to worry about instead of me."

"You sound way too happy about that."

LIZA ALREADY HAD THE CRIME scene cordoned off when Hud arrived. He waved to the deputy on guard at the falls parking lot as he got out of his patrol SUV. The coroner's van was parked next to the two police vehicles.

"The coroner just went in," the deputy told him.

He turned on his flashlight and started down the trail. Hud couldn't help thinking about his wife's siblings trying to force her to sell the family ranch. They'd been like vultures, none of them having any interest in Cardwell Ranch. All they'd wanted was the money.

Jordan had been the worst because of his New York lifestyle—and his out-of-work model wife. But Stacy and Clay had had their hands out, as well. Hud hated to think what would have happened if Dana hadn't found the new will her mother had made leaving her the ranch.

He smiled at the memory of where she'd found it. Mary Justice Cardwell had put it in her favorite old recipe book next to "Double Chocolate Brownies." The brownies had been Hud's favorite. Dana hadn't made them in all the time the two of them had been apart. When they'd gotten back together six years ago, Dana had opened the cookbook planning to surprise him with the brownies, only to be surprised herself.

Two of her siblings were back in the canyon? That had him worried even before the call from his deputy marshal that there'd been a murder. And oh, yeah, Liza had told him, Jordan Cardwell was somehow involved.

Now as he hiked into the falls, he tried to keep his temper in check. If Dana's family thought they were going to come back here and upset her—

Ahead he saw the crowd gathered at the top of the falls. He headed for the coroner.

Coroner Rupert Milligan was hugging seventy, but

you'd never know it the way he acted. Six years ago, Hud had thought the man older than God and more powerful in this county. Tall, white-haired, with a head like a buffalo, he had a gruff voice and little patience for stupidity. He'd retired as a country doctor to work as a coroner.

None of that had changed in the past six years. Just as Rupert's love for murder mysteries and forensics hadn't.

"So what do we have?" Hud asked over the roar of the falls as he joined him.

Rupert answered without even bothering to look up. "Single gunshot through the heart. Another through the lungs. High-powered rifle."

"Distance?"

"I'd say fifty yards."

"That far," he said, surprised. The killer would have needed the victim to be out in the open with no trees in the way to make such a shot. Like at the top of a water-fall. "Any idea where the shot came from?"

Rupert had been crouched beside the body. Now he finally looked up. "In case you haven't noticed, it's dark out. Once it gets daylight you can look for tracks and possibly a shell casing. And once I get the body to Bozeman for an autopsy I might be able to tell you more about the trajectory of the bullet. Offhand, I'd say the shot came from the other side of the creek, probably on the side of the mountain."

"So either it was a lucky shot or the killer had been set up and waiting," Liza said, joining them. "The killer either picked the meeting spot or was told where the victim would be."

Rupert shifted his gaze to her and frowned. Being from the old school, the coroner made no secret of the fact that he didn't hold much appreciation for women law enforcement. If he'd had his way, he would have put them all behind a desk.

Hud liked that Liza didn't seem to let him bother her. His deputy marshal's good looks could be deceiving. Small in stature, too cute for her own good and easygoing, Liza often gave criminals the idea that she was a pushover. They, however, quickly learned differently. He wondered if Jordan Cardwell thought the same thing about the deputy marshal. If so, he was in for a surprise.

"Which could mean either that the victim was expecting to meet not only Jordan Cardwell up here, but also someone he trusted," she continued. "Or—"

"Or Jordan told the killer about the meeting," Hud interjected.

Liza nodded and glanced over to the stump where Jordan was waiting. "That is always another possibility."

"One I suggest you don't forget," Hud said under his breath. "If it's all right with you, I'll take our suspect down to the office."

She nodded. "I want to wait for the crime scene techs to arrive."

Hud hadn't seen Jordan for six years. As he walked toward him, he was thinking he could have easily gone another six and not been in the least bit sorry.

"You just happen to come back to the canyon and a man dies," he said.

"Good to see you again, too, brother-in-law. I guess my invitation to the wedding must have gotten lost in the mail, huh?"

"What are you doing here, Jordan?"

"I already told your deputy marshal."

"Well, you're going to have to tell me, too. Let's get out of the woods and go to my office. You have a rifle you need to pick up before we go?"

Jordan gave him a grim, disappointed look. "No, I'm good."

THE DOOR OPENED A CRACK. "Oh, good, you're awake," Stacy said as she peered in at Dana. "I brought you some still-warm chocolate chips cookies and some milk."

"That was very thoughtful of you," Dana said, sitting up in the bed and putting her crossword puzzle aside. Earlier, before her doctor's appointment, Hud had made her a bed in the sunroom so she wouldn't have to go up the stairs—and would be where she could see most of what was going on. She patted the bed, and her sister sat down on the edge and placed the tray next to them.

"I'm just glad you let me stay and help out. It was fun baking with Hank and Mary. They are so cute. Hank looks just like a small version of Hud and Mary is the spitting image of you. Do you know…" She motioned to Dana's big belly.

"No," she said, taking a bite of cookie. "We want to be surprised. Did you find out ahead of time?"

Stacy had cautiously placed a hand on Dana's abdomen and now waited with expectation. The babies had been restless all day, kicking up a storm. She watched her sister's face light up as one of the twins gave her hand a swift kick.

Stacy laughed and pulled her hand back. "Isn't that the coolest thing ever?"

Dana nodded, studying her older sister. Stacy had changed little in appearance. She was still the pretty one. Her dark hair was chin-length, making her brown eyes the focus of her face. She'd always had that innocent look. That was probably, Dana realized with a start, why she'd been able to get away with as much as she had.

"So did you know ahead of time you were having a girl?" she asked again.

Stacy shook her head and helped herself to a cookie. "It was a surprise."

"Speaking of surprises…" She watched her sister's face. "Jordan is in town."

"Jordan?" Had Stacy known? "What is *he* doing here?"

"I thought you might know."

Stacy shook her head and looked worried. "I haven't heard from him since we were all here six years ago." She made a face. "I still feel bad about trying to force you to sell the ranch."

Dana waved that away. "It's history. The ranch is still in the family and it makes enough money that you and our brothers get to share in the profits. You know I think my lawyer did mention that he'd received notice that Jordan was divorced."

"I wonder how much of his ranch profits he has to give to Jill? That woman was such a gold digger." Stacy laughed as she realized the irony. "I should know, huh? Back then I figured if I was going to get married, I might as well get paid for it." She shook her head as if amazed by the woman she'd been. "Have you heard from Clay?"

"No." She helped herself to another cookie and sipped some of the milk. "He hasn't been cashing his checks lately. My attorney is checking into it."

"That's odd," Stacy agreed. "Well, I need to clean up the kitchen."

"Thanks so much for giving the kids their baths and getting them to bed." Mary and Hank had come in earlier to say good-night and have Dana read a book to them before bed. They'd been wearing their footie pajamas, their sweet faces scrubbed clean and shiny. They'd been excited about helping their aunt Stacy cook.

"Thank you so much for all your help," Dana said, touched by everything Stacy had done.

"I'm just glad I was here so I could." She smiled. "I didn't know how fun kids could be."

"Wait until Ella is that age. Mary loves to have tea parties and help her daddy cook."

Stacy nodded thoughtfully. "Let me know if you need anything. Knowing you, I can guess how hard it is for you to stay down like this."

Dana groaned in response. She couldn't stand the thought of another day let alone weeks like this. "Thanks for the cookies and milk. The cookies were delicious."

Stacy looked pleased as she left the room.

Chapter Four

Hud walked out with Jordan to the road, then followed him to the marshal's office. Once in the office he got his first good look at his brother-in-law. Jordan had been only two years ahead of Hud in school, three years ahead of his sister Dana. His brother-in-law had aged, but it hadn't hurt Jordan's looks. If anything the years seemed to have given him character, or at least the appearance of it.

"Why don't you have a seat and start at the beginning?" Hud said dropping into his chair behind his desk.

"I thought Liza was handling this case?"

"*Liza?* You mean Deputy Marshal Turner?" He shouldn't have been surprised Jordan was on a first-name basis with the deputy. He, of all people, understood the charm of the Justice-Cardwell genes. Dana could wrap him around her little finger and did.

"Don't think just because she's a woman that she isn't a damned good marshal," Hud said to his brother-in-law. "She's sharp and she'll nail you to the wall if you're guilty."

"If you have so much confidence in her abilities, then why are you here?"

Hud gritted his teeth. Jordan had always been dif-

ficult. At least that hadn't changed. "Several reasons.
None of which I have to explain to you. But—" He held
up a hand before Jordan could speak. "I will because I
want us to have an understanding." He ticked them off
on his fingers. "One, I'm still the marshal here. Two,
Liza has her hands full up at the site. Three, I want to
know what happened on that mountain. And four, your
sister is my wife. I don't want her hurt."

With a smile and a nod, Jordan ambled over to a
chair and sat. "Dana doesn't have anything to worry
about. Neither she nor the ranch is why I'm back in
the canyon."

"Why *are* you here?" Hud asked, snapping on the
recording machine.

"It doesn't have anything to do with family."

"But it does have something to do with Alex
Winslow."

"Alex was a good friend from high school. I didn't
kill him." Jordan sighed and looked at the ceiling for
a moment.

Hud noticed that he was no longer wearing a wedding ring. He vaguely remembered Dana mentioning
that she'd heard Jordan was divorced from his ex-model
wife, Jill. The marriage had probably ended when Jordan didn't get the proceeds from the sale of the ranch.

"If Alex was your friend, I would think you'd be interested in helping us find his killer," Hud said. "Not
to mention you're neck deep in this. Right now, you're
the number one suspect."

Jordan laughed. "Does that work on most of your
suspects?" He shook his head. "I came back because
Alex called me. He hinted that he might know something about Tanner's suicide but it was clear he didn't

want to talk about it on the phone. He said he'd share his theory with me if I came to our twenty-year high school reunion. The next time I talked to him, he sounded scared and wanted to meet at the falls. That's it."

That was a lot. Hud wasn't sure how much of it he believed. But at least he had some idea of what might have brought Jordan back to town—and it wasn't family.

"Tanner Cole committed suicide when the two of you were seniors in high school. Why would that bring you back here after all these years?"

"When your best friend commits suicide, you never stop thinking you could have done something to stop him. You need to know *why* he did it."

"Unless that person leaves a note, you never know. Tanner didn't leave a note, as I recall."

Jordan shook his head.

"Did you talk to Alex before he was shot?"

"As I told your deputy, I heard the shot, he stumbled toward me, there was another shot and he went down. All he said was the word *Shelby*. At least that's what I thought he said." Jordan shrugged. "That was it."

Hud studied him openly for a moment. "Maybe the bullets were meant for you and the killer missed."

Jordan sighed. "What are you insinuating?"

"That maybe Tanner didn't commit suicide. Weren't you the one who found his body?"

Anger fired Jordan's gaze. "He was my *best* friend. I would have taken a bullet *for* him."

"Instead, another friend of yours took the bullet tonight," Hud said. "You're telling me you came all this way, hiked into the falls in the dark, just for answers?"

"Why is that so hard for you to understand?"

"What about Alex Winslow? Don't I remember some falling-out the two of you had before you graduated?"

"It was high school. Who remembers?"

Hud nodded. "Is Stacy in the canyon for the same reason?" Stacy had been in the grade between the two of them.

"Stacy?" Jordan looked genuinely surprised. "I haven't seen or talked to her in years."

"Then you didn't know that not only is she back in the canyon, she also has a baby."

Jordan laughed. "Stacy has a *baby?* That's got to be good. Look, if that's all, I need to get some sleep."

"Once Liza allows you to, I'm sure you'll be leaving. I'd appreciate it if you didn't upset Dana before then. She's pregnant with twins and having a rough go of it."

"I'm sorry to hear that," Jordan said, sounding as if he meant it. "Don't worry, I won't be bothering my sister. Either of my sisters," he added.

"Then I guess we're done here."

A WHILE LATER, DANA HEARD HUD come in. She heard him go upstairs to check on the kids, before coming back down to her room. He smiled when he saw her still awake and came over to her side of the bed to give her a kiss.

"So everything's all right?" he asked.

"I'm the one who should be asking you that. You said there'd been a shooting?"

He nodded. "Liza's got everything under control. The crime techs are on their way from Missoula." He sounded tired.

"Stacy kept a plate of dinner for you. She made chicken, baked potatoes and corn," Dana said. "Then she and kids baked chocolate chip cookies." She motioned to the cookies on the tray next to the bed.

Hud gave her a who-knew-she-could-cook look and took one of the cookies.

Who knew indeed? Dana couldn't believe the change in her sister. She felt horribly guilty for not trusting it. But even Stacy was capable of changing, right? Having a baby did that to a person. But Stacy?

Unfortunately, the jury was still out—given her sister's past.

"Did she mention how long she's staying?" Hud asked, not meeting her gaze.

"She was planning to leave earlier, but I asked her to stay. I'm sure she'll be leaving in the morning."

Hud nodded. She could tell he would be glad when Stacy was gone. Dana couldn't blame him. Her sister had hurt them both. But she desperately wanted to believe Stacy had changed. For Ella's sake.

Unfortunately, like her husband, Dana had a niggling feeling that Stacy wasn't being completely honest about the real reason she'd come to the ranch.

EXHAUSTED, JORDAN WENT BACK TO his cabin, locked the door and fell into bed with the intention of sleeping the rest of the day.

Unfortunately, Deputy Marshal Liza Turner had other plans for him.

"What do you want?" he said when he opened the cabin door a little after eleven o'clock that morning to find her standing outside. He leaned a hip into the doorjamb and crossed his arms as he took her in.

"What do I want? Sleep, more money, better hours, breakfast."

"I can't help you with most of that, but I could use food. I'll buy."

She smiled. "I know a place that serves breakfast all day. We can eat and talk."

"No murder talk until I've had coffee."

"Agreed."

Liza drove them to the upper mountain. The huge unpaved parking lots sat empty. None of the lifts moved on the mountain except for the gondolas that rocked gently in the breeze.

"It's like a ghost town up here," he commented as they got out of her patrol SUV.

"I like the quiet. Good place to talk. Most everything is closed still. Fortunately, there are enough locals that a few places stay open."

The café was small and nearly empty. Liza led him outside to a table under an umbrella. The sun was low to the south, but still warm enough it was comfortable outside. A waitress brought them coffee while they looked at the menu.

Jordan ordered ham and eggs, hashbrowns and whole wheat toast.

"I'll have the same," Liza said and handed back the menu. As soon as the waitress was out of earshot, she said, "You didn't mention last night that you and the victim were no longer friends at the end of your high school years."

"So you spoke with Hud." He looked toward the mountains where snow dusted the peaks, making them gleam blinding bright. "It was a stupid disagreement over a woman, all right? Just high school stuff."

She nodded, not buying it. "What girl?"

"I don't even remember."

Liza's look called him a liar, but she let it go. "I'm still confused why he contacted *you*. He must have had other friends locally he would have talked to."

"Obviously he must have talked to someone locally. One of them knew where he was going last night and killed him." Jordan said nothing as the waitress served their breakfasts. He picked up his fork. "Look, do we have to talk about this while we eat? I feel like I got him killed."

"You can't blame yourself, or worse, try to take the law into your own hands." She eyed him for a long moment. "Why would I suspect that's what you're planning to do?"

He chuckled. "If you talked to my brother-in-law he would have told you that I'm not that ambitious. Anyway, you're the deputy marshal. I'm sure you'll find his killer."

She took a bite of toast, chewed and swallowed before she said, "You contacted Tanner's girlfriend from his senior year in high school."

Jordan took her measure. "Why, Liza, you've been checking up on me. I contacted Shelby before I went up to the falls last night. She said she had nothing to say to me about Tanner. That was high school and so far back, she barely remembers."

"You didn't believe her?" Liza asked between bites.

Jordan laughed. "High school was Shelby's glory days. Just check out our yearbook. She is on every page either as president or queen of something. Not to mention she was dating Tanner Cole, the most popular guy in school. She was in her element. I'd bet those were the best days of her life and that nothing she has done since will ever compare."

Liza considered that for a long moment before she asked, "So you talked to Shelby before last night. Before the only word Alex got out after he was shot was her name?"

"Like I said, she and Tanner dated."

"When you talked to Shelby, did you mention Alex or where you were meeting him?"

He gave her an exasperated look. "Do you really think I'm that stupid? Alex was acting terrified. I wasn't about to say anything until I talked to him."

"And yet you called Shelby."

"Yeah. I just told her I was in the area as if I was here for the twenty-year reunion and worked Tanner into the conversation. I didn't realize then that anything I might do could put anyone in danger, including her."

"That's so noble. But I thought you didn't like her. In fact, I thought you were instrumental in breaking up her and Tanner."

He shook his head and took a bite of his breakfast. "You're determined to ruin my appetite, aren't you?"

"Is it true?"

"I couldn't stand Shelby and that bunch she ran with. But you're wrong. I had nothing to do with breaking her and Tanner up, no matter what Hud thinks, as I'm sure that's where you got your information."

Liza lifted a brow. "You weren't the one who snitched on her?"

"Wasn't me." He met her gaze. "Why keep questioning me if you aren't going to believe anything I say?"

"I don't want you involved in my investigation," she said. "That includes asking about Tanner among your old friends—and enemies."

He smiled. "What makes you think I have enemies?"

She smiled in answer as she smeared huckleberry jam on a piece of her toast.

He watched her eat for a few moments. He liked a woman who ate well and said as much.

"Does that line work on women?" she asked.

He laughed. "Every time."

They finished their breakfast in the quiet of the upper mountain. She was right about it being peaceful up here. He liked it. But once winter came, all that would change. The parking lots would be packed, all the lifts would be running as well as the gondola. The mountain would be dotted with skiers and boarders, the restaurants and resorts full. He recalled the sounds of people, the clank of machinery, the array of bright-colored skiwear like a rainbow across Lone Mountain.

Tanner had loved it when Big Sky took on its winter wonderland persona. He'd loved to ski, had started at the age of three like a lot of the kids who grew up in the shadow of Lone Mountain.

With a start, Jordan found himself looking high up on the peak, remembering one of the last days he and Tanner had skied the winter of their senior year. Tanner had always been gutsy, but that day he'd talked Alex and him into going into an out-of-bounds area.

They hadn't gone far when Tanner had gone off a cornice. The cornice had collapsed, causing a small avalanche that had almost killed him.

"Hey, man. You have a death wish?" Alex had asked Tanner when they'd skied down to find him half-buried in the snow.

Tanner had laughed it off. "Takes more than that to kill me."

"I THOUGHT YOU'D BE HAPPIER down here," Hud said as he opened the curtains in the sunroom. "You can leave the door open so you can see everything that is going on."

Dana shot him a look. Seeing everything that was going on was his not-so-subtle way of saying he wanted her to keep an eye on her sister.

They'd all gathered around her bed after breakfast. Stacy hadn't made any attempt to leave. Just the opposite, she seemed to be finding more things she wanted to do before she and Ella packed for the rest of their trip.

"Is there any chance you could stay another day or so?" Dana asked her now as Stacy picked up her breakfast tray to take to the kitchen.

Her sister stopped and looked up in surprise. Her face softened as if she was touched by Dana's offer. "I'd love to. I can cook and help with the kids. Hud has this murder investigation—"

"My deputy marshal is handling all of that," Hud interrupted, shooting Dana a what-could-you-be-thinking? look. "Plus the crime techs are down from Missoula. I am more than capable of taking care of Dana and the kids and—"

Dana had been holding Ella since finishing her breakfast. She quickly interrupted him. "Stacy, that would be great if you can. I know Hud won't mind the help and I love having you and Ella here."

Her husband sent her a withering look. She ignored it and looked instead into Ella's adorable face.

"Is Auntie Stacy going to stay, Mommy?" Mary asked excitedly.

"Yes, for a few more days. Would you like that?" Both children cheered.

"Auntie Stacy is going to show us how to make clay,"

Hank said. "You have to put it in the oven and then paint it."

Stacy shrugged when Dana looked at her. "I found a recipe on the internet. I thought they'd like that."

"That was very thoughtful," she said and shot her husband a see?-everything-is-fine look. "I know Hud will want to check in with the murder investigation, and there are animals to feed."

He tried to stare her down, but Dana had grown up with three siblings. Having to fight for what she wanted had made her a strong, determined woman.

"Fine," Hud said as he left the room. "Stacy, if you need me, Dana has my number. I have animals to feed."

"He'll check in with Liza," Dana said. "He can pretend otherwise, but he won't be able to stay away from this case."

"Are you sure it's all right if I stay?" Stacy asked. "Hud doesn't seem—"

"He's just being territorial," she said. "He can't stand the idea that anyone might think he can't take care of his family." Dana reached for her sister's hand and squeezed it. "I'm glad you and Ella are here."

LIZA FIGURED JORDAN CARDWELL had lied to her at least twice during breakfast.

"I need to know everything you can remember that led up to Tanner's death," she said when they'd finished their breakfast and the waitress had cleared away their plates and refilled their coffee cups.

The scent of pine blew down on the breeze from the mountain peaks. She breathed in the fall day and pulled out her notebook. They still had the café deck to themselves and the sun felt heavenly after so little sleep last night.

"We were seniors." Jordan shrugged. "Not much was going on."

"Who did Tanner date after his breakup with Shelby?"

"A couple of different girls."

"Who was he dating in the weeks or days before he died?" she asked.

"Brittany Cooke." The way he said it gave him away.

"You liked her?" she asked with interest.

His shrug didn't fool her.

"You used to date her?"

He laughed, meeting her gaze. "You got all that out of a shrug?"

"Who were *you* dating at the time?" she asked.

"I don't see what—"

"Humor me."

"I can't remember."

She laughed and leaned back in her chair to eye him. "You don't remember who you were dating the spring of your senior year? Give me a break."

"I wasn't dating anyone, really. It's a small community, cliques. There weren't a lot of options unless you dated someone from Bozeman. I was just anxious to graduate and get out of here."

"Shelby and Brittany were in one of these cliques?"

"Not Brittany. Brittany and Shelby got along, but she was never really one of them. But Shelby, yeah. She was the leader of the mean girls—you know the type. Too much money, too much everything."

Liza knew the type only too well. "So what happened when Brittany went out with Tanner?"

"I'm sure Shelby would deny it, but her and her group of friends closed Brittany out."

"What did Tanner think about that?"

"He thought it was funny. Believe me, that wasn't why he killed himself. Don't get me wrong, Tanner liked Shelby. He went with her a lot longer than any other girl. But once he found out she'd been trying to get pregnant to trap him, it was all over. He wasn't ready to settle down. He'd worked two jobs all through high school while getting good grades so he could do some of the things he'd always wanted to do. Both of us couldn't wait to travel."

"And get out of the canyon," Liza said.

"Tanner not as much as me. He would have come back to the family ranch. He was a cowboy."

"He wasn't from Big Sky resort money?"

"Naw, his folks have a ranch down the canyon. They do okay, just like everyone else who still ranches around here. As my sister is fond of saying, it's a lifestyle more than a paying career. Tanner *loved* that lifestyle, was happiest in a saddle and not afraid of hard work."

"He sounds like a nice, sensible young man."

"He was." Jordan looked away toward the mountains for a long moment. "He worked a lot of odd jobs throughout high school. That's how he ended up at that cabin on the mountain. He talked his folks into letting him stay there because it was closer to school. He traded watching the landowner's construction equipment for the small cabin where he lived that spring."

"He didn't want to live at home?"

Jordan grinned. "Not his senior year. His parents were strict, like all parents when you're that age. Tanner wanted to be on his own and his folks were okay with it."

"So who were the mean girls?"

"Shelby, the leader. Tessa, her closest ally. Whitney. Ashley. They were the inner circle."

"And Brittany?"

"She was always on the fringe. Last I heard Brittany had married Lee Peterson and they have a bunch of kids. I think I heard they live in Meadow Village. Shelby married Wyatt Iverson. She'd started dating him after she and Tanner broke up. Wyatt's father was a contractor who built a lot of the huge vacation homes. It was his maintenance cabin where Tanner stayed with his equipment." He stopped, a faraway look coming to his gaze. "Shelby has a yoga studio near the Gallatin River."

For a life he'd put behind him, Jordan certainly knew a lot about the players, Liza thought as she closed her notebook.

Chapter Five

Yogamotion was in a narrow complex built of log and stone, Western-style. Liza pushed open the door to find the inside brightly painted around walls of shiny mirrors.

According to the schedule she'd seen on the door, the next class wasn't for a couple of hours. A lithe young woman sat behind a large desk in a room off to the side. She was talking on a cell phone, but looked up as the door closed behind Liza.

"You should be getting the check any day. I'm sorry, but I have to go," she said into the phone and slowly snapped it shut, never taking her eyes off the deputy marshal.

"Shelby Iverson?"

As the woman got to her feet she took in Liza's attire, the boots, jeans and tan uniform shirt with the silver star on it. "I'm Shelby *Durran-Iverson*."

"Liza Turner, deputy marshal." Big Sky was small enough that Liza had seen Shelby around. The canyon resort was situated such that there were pockets of development, some pricier than others depending on where you lived.

Shelby lived in a large single-family home on the

north side of the mountain on the way to Mountain Village, while Liza lived in a condo in Meadow Village. She and Shelby didn't cross paths a lot.

"I'd like to ask you a few questions," the deputy said.

"Me?" The catch in her throat was merely for effect. Shelby Durran-Iverson had been expecting a visit from the marshal's office. Everyone within fifty miles would have heard about Alex Winslow's murder at the falls last night. Word would have spread through Big Sky like a fast-moving avalanche.

Liza had to wonder though, why Shelby thought *she* would be questioned. "It's about the shooting last night."

"I don't know anything about it," she said.

"But you knew Alex."

"Sure. Everyone from around here knew him."

"You went to high school with him?" Liza asked pulling her notebook and pen from her pocket.

"Do I need a lawyer?"

"You tell me. Did you shoot Alex?"

"No." Shelby sounded shocked that Liza would even suggest such a thing.

"Then I guess you don't need a lawyer. I just need to ask you a few questions so I can find the person who did shoot him."

"I still can't see how *I* can help." But she motioned Liza to a chair and took her own behind the desk again. Liza could tell that Shelby was hoping to learn more about the murder, getting more information out of her than she provided.

Settling into a chair across the desk from her, Liza studied Shelby. She was a shapely blonde who looked as if she just stepped out of a magazine ad. Her hair was pulled up in a sleek ponytail. Everything about her seemed planned for maximum effect from her makeup to her jewelry and the clothes on her back. She wore a flattering coral velvet designer sweatsuit that brought out the blue of her eyes and accentuated her well-toned body.

"I understand you used to date Tanner Cole," Liza said.

"*Tanner?* I thought you were here about Alex?"

"Did you date Alex, too?"

"No." She shook her head, the ponytail sweeping back and forth. "You're confusing me." She flashed a perfect-toothed smile, clearly a girl who'd had braces.

"I don't want to confuse you. So you dated Tanner how long?"

She frowned, still confused apparently. "Till just before Christmas of our senior year, I guess."

"But the two of you broke up?"

"I can't understand how that—"

Liza gave her one of her less-than-perfect-toothed smiles. She'd been born with a slight gap between her front teeth that her parents had found cute and she had never gotten around to changing. "Humor me. I actually know what I'm doing."

Shelby sighed, making it clear she had her doubts about that. "Fine. Yes, I dated Tanner, I don't remember when we broke up."

"Or why?"

The yoga instructor's eyes narrowed in challenge. "No."

"Here's the thing, I'm trying to understand why Tanner killed himself and why now one of his friends has been murdered."

"I'm sure there is no possible connection," Shelby

said with a mocking laugh as if now she knew Liza
didn't know what she was doing.

"So Tanner didn't kill himself over you?"

"No!"

"So you weren't that serious?"

Shelby fumbled for words for a moment. "It was high
school. It seemed serious at the time."

"To you. Or Tanner?"

"To both of us." She sounded defensive and realizing
it, gave a small laugh. "Like I said, it was *high school*."

Liza looked down at her notebook. "Let's see, by that
spring, Tanner was dating Brittany Cooke? Wasn't she
a friend of yours?"

Shelby's mouth tightened. "Tanner was sowing
his oats before graduation. I can assure you he wasn't
serious about Brittany."

"Oh? Did she tell you that?"

"She didn't have to. She wasn't Tanner's type."
Shelby straightened several things on her desk that
didn't need straightening. "If that's all, I really need to
get back to work."

"I forgot what you said. *Did* you date Alex?"

"No, and I'd lost track of him since high school."

"That's right, he'd moved down to Bozeman and had
only recently returned to Big Sky for the class reunion?"

"I assume that's why he came back."

"You didn't talk to him?" Liza asked.

Shelby thought for a moment. More than likely she
was carefully considering her next answer. If Liza had
Alex's cell phone in her possession, she would know
who he called right before his death—and who'd called
him.

"I might have talked to him since I'm the reunion

chairwoman. I talked to a lot of people. I really can't remember."

"That's strange since you talked to Alex five times in two days, the last three of those calls just hours before he was killed."

Shelby didn't look quite so put-together. "I told you, it was about the reunion. I talked to a lot of people."

"Are you telling me he didn't ask you about Tanner's alleged suicide?" Liza said.

"*Alleged* suicide?"

"Apparently, Alex had some questions about Tanner's death."

Shelby shook her head. "I might have heard that, but I wouldn't have taken anything Alex said seriously." She leaned forward and lowered her voice even though they were the only two people there. "I heard he had some sort of breakdown." She leaned back and lifted a brow as if to say that covered it.

"Hmmm. I hadn't heard that." Liza jotted down a note. "Whom did you hear this from?"

"I don't—"

"Recall. Maybe one of your friends?"

Shelby shook her head. "I really can't remember. I'm sure you can find out if there was any truth to it."

Liza smiled. "Yes, I can. What about Brittany?"

"What about her?" Shelby asked stiffly.

"Do you still see her?"

"Big Sky is a small community. You're bound to see everyone at some point," Shelby answered noncommittally. "She and her husband, Lee Peterson, own a ski shop up on the mountain. Now I really do need to get to work," she said, rising to her feet.

"Did you see Tanner the night he died?"

"No. As you are apparently aware, we had broken up. He was dating Brittany. If anyone knows why he killed himself, she would, don't you think?"

"Even though she and Tanner weren't that serious about each other?"

Shelby's jaw muscle bunched and her blue eyes fired with irritation. "If she doesn't know, then who would?"

"Good question. Maybe Alex Winslow. But then he isn't talking, is he?" Liza said as she closed her notebook and got to her feet. "One more question. Why would the last word Alex Winslow would say be your name?"

All the color washed from her face. She sat back down, leaning heavily on her desk. "I have no idea."

AFTER BREAKFAST, JORDAN WENT back to his cabin and crashed for a while. He figured Liza would be keeping an eye on him. Not that he knew what to do next. He couldn't just hang out in this cabin, that was for sure. But he'd been serious about not wanting to put anyone else in danger.

When he woke up, he realized he was hungry again. It was still early since the sun hadn't sunk behind Lone Mountain. According to his cell phone, it was a quarter past three in the afternoon.

He found a small sandwich shop in Meadow Village, ordered a turkey and cheese and took a seat by the window overlooking the golf course. Lone Mountain gleamed in the background, a sight that brought back too many memories. There'd been a time when he'd told himself he'd left here because he didn't want to be a rancher. But coming back here now, he realized a lot of his need to leave and stay gone had to do with Tanner's suicide.

When the waitress brought out his sandwich, he asked if he could get it to go. He followed her to the counter and was waiting when he heard a bell tinkle over the door and turned to see someone he recognized coming through.

With a silent curse, he put a name to the face. Tessa Ryerson. She had already spotted him and something about her expression gave him the crazy idea that she didn't just happen in here. She'd come looking for him.

Before he could react, the waitress brought out his sandwich in a brown paper bag and handed it to him. He dug out the cost of the sandwich and a generous tip and handed it to the server, before turning to Tessa.

She had stopped just a couple of feet from him, waiting while he paid. When he turned to her, he saw that she looked much like she had twenty years ago when the two of them had dated. She wore her light brown hair as she had in high school, shoulder length and wavy, no bangs. A hair band held it back from her face.

She seemed thinner, a little more gaunt in the face, than she had the last time he'd seen her. He recalled that she'd always struggled to keep her weight down. Apparently, she'd mastered the problem.

He couldn't help noticing that her ring finger was bare. Hadn't he heard that she'd gone through a bad divorce from Danny Spring? Two years ahead of them in school, the guy had been a jerk. Jordan recalled being surprised when he'd heard that she'd married him.

"Jordan," Tessa said a little too brightly. "Imagine running into you here."

"Imagine that," he said, now sure the only reason

she'd come in here, crazy or not, was to see him. So did that mean she'd followed him? Or had she just been looking for him?

"Oh, are you getting your sandwich to go?" she asked, sounding disappointed as she glanced at the bag in his hand as if just now noticing it. "I missed lunch and I hate eating alone. Would you mind staying?"

How could he say no even if he'd wanted to? Anyway, he was curious about what she wanted. "Sure, go ahead and order. I'll get us a table."

"Great."

He took a seat away from the girl working behind the counter, positioning himself so he could watch Tessa while she ordered. She dug nervously in her purse, paid for a small salad and a bottled water, then joined him at the table.

"So you came for the reunion," she said, smiling as she unscrewed the lid on her water bottle.

He smiled at that and dug his sandwich out of the bag and took a bite.

"Wow, it's been so long."

"Twenty years," he said between bites.

"I guess you heard about Danny and me." She sighed. "But I've put it behind me."

Too bad the look in her eyes said otherwise. He suspected the slightest thing could set her off if asked about her marriage. Unfortunately, he could remember how he was right after Jill had left him. He didn't want to go there again.

"So wasn't that awful about Alex?" she said. "Were you really there?"

He gave her points for getting right to what she really

wanted to talk to him about. He nodded and took another bite of his sandwich. She hadn't touched her salad.

"When I heard, I just couldn't believe it. How horrible. Do they know who shot him?" she asked when he didn't answer. "I heard it could have been a stray bullet from a hunter."

"Really?" he said. "I heard it was murder. Someone wanted to shut Alex up."

"Who told you that?" she cried.

He said nothing for a moment, letting her squirm. "The state crime lab trucks have been up at the falls since last night looking for evidence to track them to the killer. I thought you would have heard."

Tessa fiddled with her water bottle, looking worried. "Why would anyone want to kill Alex?"

He shrugged. "Probably because he'd been asking a lot of questions about Tanner's suicide. But you'd know better about that than I would."

"Me?"

"I'm sure Alex talked to you." He wasn't sure of anything except that he was rattling her. "If you know something, I'd suggest you talk to Deputy Marshal Liza Turner. Alex was murdered and there is an investigation into Tanner's death, as well. It's all going to come out."

"I don't know *anything.*" She squeezed her plastic water bottle so hard it crackled loudly and water shot up and out over the table. She jumped up and grabbed for a stack of napkins.

He watched her nervously wipe up the spilled water, almost feeling guilty for upsetting her. "Then I guess you have nothing to worry about. But I wonder if Alex said the same thing."

"This is all so upsetting." She sounded close to tears.

He reached across the table and put a hand on hers. "Tessa—"

"Please, don't," she said, snatching back her hand. "I told you. I don't know anything."

He put down his sandwich to study her. Why had she come looking for him? Why was she so scared? "You and Shelby have always been thick as thieves. What don't I know about Alex's death? Or Tanner's, for that matter."

She shook her head. "How would I know? Shelby wasn't even dating Tanner then."

"No, but she'd conned you into breaking up with Alex to go out with me. I thought you were just playing hard to get when you wanted to always double date with Brittany and Tanner. I should have known Shelby put you up to spying on him."

"I don't know what you're talking about," she said. "But I do remember you didn't mind double dating. It was Brittany you wanted to be with. Not me." She got to her feet, hitting the table and spilling some of her salad.

"Brittany," he said under his breath. "Thanks for reminding me of that prank you and your friend Shelby pulled on her." It was straight out of a Stephen King novel.

Tessa crossed her toned arms over her flat chest, her expression defiant. He'd expected her to stomp off, but she didn't. Whatever the reason that she'd wanted to see him, she hadn't got what she'd come for apparently.

That spring of their senior year was coming back to him after years of fighting to forget it. Hadn't he had a bad feeling he couldn't shake even before Alex had called him? "Did Shelby send you to find me?" He let out a laugh. "Just like in high school. What is it she wants to know, Tessa?"

"I have no idea what you mean."

He laughed. "Still doing her dirty work even after all these years."

Tessa snatched up her water bottle from the table with one hand, the untouched salad with the other. "I know what you think of me."

"I think you're too smart to keep letting Shelby run your life."

She laughed at that. "Run my life? Don't you mean *ruin* my life? She practically forced me to marry Danny Spring. It wasn't until later that I found out her husband was trying to buy some land Danny owned and thought my marriage would get it for Wyatt." She smiled. "It did."

"Then what are you doing still being friends with her?" he demanded.

"*Seriously?* Because it's much worse to be Shelby's enemy, haven't you realized that yet? My life isn't the only one she's destroyed. Clearly, you have forgotten what she's like."

"No, I don't think so. I know what she did to Tanner."

"Do you?" she challenged.

"She got pregnant to trap him into marrying her. If she hadn't miscarried, he probably would have married her for the kid's sake." Something in Tessa's expression stopped him. "She did have a miscarriage, didn't she? Or did she lie about that, as well?"

Tessa looked away for a moment.

Jordan felt his heart drop. *My life isn't the only one she's destroyed.* The thought came at him with such force, he knew it had been in the back of his mind for a long time.

"She didn't do something to that baby to get back at Tanner, did she?" he asked, voicing his fear.

"I have to go," Tessa said, glancing toward the parking lot.

He followed her gaze, seeing her fear as a white SUV cruised slowly past. He recognized Shelby Durran-Iverson behind the wheel. She sped up when she saw Tessa hurry out of the sandwich shop, barely missing her as she drove away.

Jordan stared after both of them for a moment before he wrapped up his sandwich. He'd lost his appetite. Worse, he wasn't sure what his best friend would have done if he'd found out Shelby hadn't miscarried early in the pregnancy, but waited as long as she could, then aborted his baby to hurt him.

He realized it was possible Tanner really had killed himself.

Chapter Six

The ski shop Brittany Cooke Peterson and her husband Lee owned on the mountain was still closed for the season.

But Liza found her at the couple's condo in Meadow Village. Brittany answered the door wearing a black-and-white polka-dot apron over a T-shirt and jeans. Her feet were bare and her dark hair in disarray. She brushed a long curly lock back from her face, leaving a dusting of flour on her cheekbone. In the background a 1960s hit played loudly. As Brittany's brown eyes widened to see the deputy sheriff at her door, Liza caught the warm, wonderful scent of freshly-baked cookies.

"Don't touch that pan, it's hot," Brittany said over her shoulder after opening the door.

"Did I catch you in the middle of something?" Liza asked facetiously.

Brittany laughed. "Not at all."

"Mommy, Jake stuck his finger in the icing," called a young female voice from the back of the large two-story condo.

Brittany wiped her hands on her apron. "Come on in. We're baking iced pumpkin cookies."

Liza followed the young woman through a toy-cluttered living room and into a kitchen smelling of cinnamon and pumpkin.

Three small children balanced on chairs around a kitchen island covered in flour and dirty baking bowls and utensils. One of the children, the only boy, had icing smudged on the side of his cheek. Brittany licked her thumb pad and wiped the icing from the boy's face, took an icing-dripping spoon from one girl and snatched a half-eaten cookie from the other girl as if it was all in a day's work.

The two girls who Liza realized were identical twins appeared to be about five and were wearing aprons that matched their mother's. The boy had a dish towel wrapped around his neck like a bandana. He was a year or so younger than the girls.

"You'd better have a cookie," Brittany said as she finished slipping warm ones from a cookie sheet onto a cooling rack.

Liza took one of the tall stools at the counter, but declined a cookie.

"Just a little icing on them, Courtney," her mother said to the girl who had the spoon again and was dribbling thin white icing over each cookie as if making a masterpiece. The other girl watched, practically drooling as her sister slowly iced the warm cookies. "Okay, enough sugar for one day. Go get cleaned up." They jumped down and raced toward the stairs. "And don't argue!" she called after them.

With a sigh, Brittany glanced around the messy kitchen, then plopped down on a stool at the counter and took one of the cookies before turning her attention on Liza. "Sure you don't want one?" she asked between bites. "They aren't bad."

"They smell delicious, but I'm fine."

"You didn't come by for cookies," Brittany said. "This is about Alex, isn't it?" She shook her head, her expression one of sadness. "I heard it was a hunter."

"A hunter?"

"You know, someone poaching at night, a stray bullet. It had to be. No one would want to hurt Alex. He was a sweetheart. Everyone liked him."

"Not everyone," Liza said.

Brittany turned solemn. "So it *was* murder. That's the other rumor circulating this morning." She shook her head.

"Any idea who didn't think he was a sweetheart?"

"No one I can think of."

"What about Tanner Cole?"

Brittany blinked. "Even if he came back from the dead, he wouldn't have hurt Alex. They were friends."

Liza smiled. She liked the woman's sense of humor. "Do you know why Tanner killed himself?"

"No. I suppose someone told you that Tanner and I were dating at the time." Brittany chuckled as she realized whom. "Shelby. Of course."

"She did mention that if anyone knew, it would be you. Did Tanner seem depressed?"

"Far from it. He was excited about graduating. He had all these plans for what he was going to do. I think he already had his bags packed."

"He was planning to leave Big Sky?"

"Oh, yeah. He'd been saving his money for years. He wanted to backpack around Europe before college. He had a scholarship to some big college back east."

"What about you?"

"I was headed for Montana State University."

"Weren't you upset that he was leaving?"

She shook her head as she helped herself to another cookie. Upstairs, Liza could hear the kids squabbling over the water and towels. "It wasn't like that between me and Tanner. I liked him. A lot. But I knew from the get-go that it wasn't serious."

"Had it been serious between him and Shelby?"

Brittany stopped chewing for a moment. She sighed and let out a chuckle. "If you talk to Shelby it was. She was planning to marry him, apparently. She loved his parents' ranch and used to talk about when she and Tanner lived on the place, what their lives were going to be like."

"She must have been upset when he broke it off and started dating you."

Brittany laughed. "Livid. But Tanner told me he'd just gone through a scare with her. She'd apparently gotten pregnant."

"On purpose?"

"Tanner thought so. He said he'd dodged a bullet when she miscarried…" Brittany seemed to realize what she'd said. "So to speak. Anyway, he didn't trust her after that, said he didn't want anything to do with her. They broke up right before Christmas. She'd been so sure he would be putting an engagement ring under the tree for her."

"How could Shelby have thought that was going to happen?" Liza asked. "Surely she knew what Tanner was planning to do once they graduated."

"Sure, she knew, but Shelby was so used to getting what she wanted, I think she'd just convinced herself it was going to happen."

"Maybe she thought a baby would be the tipping point," Liza suggested.

"And it probably would have been. Tanner loved kids. He wanted a bunch when he settled down. If she had been pregnant, I still don't think he would have married her, but he would have stuck around to help raise his child. He was that kind of guy. But he was over Shelby. Nothing could have made him go back to her."

"Did she know that?" Liza asked.

Brittany broke a cookie in half and played in the icing for a moment. "I think she did. She really was heartbroken. She cried hysterically at the funeral. I'd never seen her like that. I actually felt sorry for her."

"But you didn't feel sorry enough not to go out with Tanner."

Brittany shrugged. "It was high school. Tanner asked me out. He was a nice guy and a lot of fun. Shelby knew it wasn't serious. She didn't blame me."

"But she did Tanner?"

Brittany smiled. "Let me put it this way. If Shelby was the kind to make voodoo dolls and stick pins in them, she would have had one with Tanner's name on it. But she moved on quick enough. Tanner was barely in the ground before she was dating Wyatt Iverson. One thing about Shelby, she seems to bounce back pretty fast."

"Wyatt Iverson of Iverson Construction?" Liza said. "Isn't that the same construction company that Tanner was working for at the time of his death?"

Brittany nodded and got up to go to the bottom of the stairs to yell up at the kids to quit fighting. When she came back she began to clean up the kitchen. "Wyatt was four years ahead of us in school, so I didn't really know him. But later that summer his father went bankrupt, shot Harris Lancaster and went to prison. Malcolm was never the same after that, I guess. He died in a boating accident. At least that's what they called it. He drowned up on Canyon Ferry. Everyone suspected he killed himself. I've gotten to know Wyatt a little since then. He never got over what happened with his father. That's one reason he's worked so hard to get the construction company going again." She looked up. "Sorry, that's probably a whole lot more than you wanted to hear."

"You like Wyatt."

Brittany smiled at that. "*Like* might be a little strong. He and Shelby are cut from the same cloth. Both go after what they want and the rest be damned." She frowned. "Why all the questions about Tanner?"

"Tanner was Alex's friend."

"And now they're both dead," Brittany said with a nod.

"With all Tanner's plans, he doesn't sound like someone who would commit suicide before graduation. Was anything else going on in his life that you knew of? Maybe with his parents, his friends?"

Brittany shook her head. "His parents are still happily married and still live on the ranch. His friends were fine—well, that is, they were until last night." She sighed. "There was the vandalism, though."

"*Vandalism?*" Liza asked.

"Tanner was staying in the cabin at the construction site in payment for watching over Malcolm Iverson's equipment. There was a party at the cabin one night. The next morning, Malcolm discovered his equipment had been vandalized. Tanner blamed himself."

"Enough to kill himself?"

"I didn't think so at the time. Wyatt didn't even blame Tanner. The party hadn't been his idea in the first place. Tanner was really responsible, but everyone showed up with beer and things must have gotten out of hand. But who knows. Maybe Tanner was taking it harder than any of us knew. Wyatt talked his father into letting Tanner stay at the cabin even after the vandalism. So I really don't think that had anything to do with Tanner's death."

"Well, thank you for the information," Liza said.

"It's kind of strange though. I heard Jordan Cardwell was back in the canyon—and that he was at the falls when Alex was shot?"

"Why is that strange if they were friends?"

"Because he and Alex had a huge falling-out the night of the party."

Liza felt her pulse quicken. "Over what?"

"I never knew. I just remember Tanner refused to take sides. He said they'd work it out."

"Did they?"

"Not that I know of. Jordan left right after graduation and seldom came back. I'm not sure he and Alex ever spoke again."

"Could it have been over a girl?"

Brittany laughed. "Isn't it always?"

"So who would that girl have been?"

"If I had to guess, I'd say Tessa Ryerson. Shelby's BFF."

Liza laughed. "Best friend forever? Is that still true?"

Brittany nodded and crossed her fingers. "Shelby and Tessa, they're like this and always have been. I was surprised when Jordan went out with Tessa since he never could stand Shelby."

DANA HAD DOZED OFF FOR A WHILE, she realized. She woke to find Hud lying on the bed next to her. Listening, she could hear the sound of their children's voices coming from the kitchen along with that of her sister's. She placed a hand on her stomach, felt her two babies and tried to relax. Nothing seemed to be amiss and yet, when she'd awakened...

"What's wrong?" she asked, turning her head to look at her husband.

Hud was staring at the ceiling. "You're going to think I'm crazy."

"I've never thought you were anything but completely sane in all instances," she joked.

"I'm serious," he said, rolling over on his side to look at her.

She saw the worry etched in his handsome face. "What?"

"You aren't going to want to hear this."

"Hud!"

"Something's wrong," he said. "I feel it."

She sighed. "Your marshal intuition again?" She felt her eyes widen, her heartbeat kicking up a notch. "About the murder investigation?"

"It's your sister."

She groaned and, shaking her head, turned to look at the ceiling. "What are you saying?"

"Have you noticed the way she is with the baby?" he demanded, keeping his voice down even though the bedroom door was closed.

Dana hadn't noticed. Usually when her sister brought the baby in, she would hand Ella to her to hold.

"It's as if she has never changed a diaper," Hud was saying.

"She's probably nervous because you're watching her. She's new at this."

He shook his head. "She stares at Ella, I swear, as if she's never seen her before. Not just that," he rushed on. "She arrived with hardly any clothes for the baby and when she came back from buying baby food, I asked her what Ella's favorite was and she said carrots. You should have seen her trying to feed Ella carrots—"

"Stop. Do you realize how ridiculous you sound?" She'd turned to look at him again. "I repeat, what are you *saying*?"

Hud clamped his mouth shut for a moment, his eyes dark. "Okay, I'll just say it. I don't think that baby is hers. In fact, I don't even think the baby's name is Ella. That baby quilt has the name Katie stitched on it."

"Okay, you are *crazy*," Dana said. "The quilt is probably one she picked up at a secondhand store or a friend lent it to her."

"A friend? Has she received even one phone call since she's been here?" He shook his head. "No, that's because your sister doesn't have friends. She never has."

"You don't know that she hasn't made friends the past six years."

"How could she? She moves around all the time. At least that's her story. And what does she do for money, huh?"

"She didn't go to college or learn a trade so of course she has a hard time supporting herself." Dana knew she was grasping at any explanation, but she couldn't stop herself. "One look at Stacy and you can see she doesn't have much. It's probably the best she can do right now. And you know babies can change their food likes and dislikes in an afternoon. As for diapering…"

Hud shook his head stubbornly.

"Is she helping with the kids?"

"Sure, she seems right at home with a four- and five-year-old." He sighed. "I still have a hard time trusting Stacy."

"I know. She stole five years from us, breaking us up with one of her lies so I understand why you would question everything about her now." Dana didn't want to admit that she had felt the same way around her sister. But when she saw her sister with Ella—

"Okay," Hud said. "After dinner I might check in with Liza and see how the investigation is going." He placed a large hand on her belly and waited for their twins to move as if needing reassurance.

She could see that it was hell for him having a murder investigation going on while he was home playing Candy Land and Old Maid. But she saw something else in his expression, as well. "You're going to your office to do more than check in, aren't you? You're going to investigate my sister."

"I just want to do some checking on her. Just to relieve my mind."

She knew there would be no stopping him no matter what she said. "I want to get to know my niece. After everything that has happened between us and Stacy, it wouldn't take much for us to never see her or Ella again."

"If Ella isn't her baby—"

"You're wrong. So go ahead and see what you can find out."

He bent down to kiss her before getting to his feet. "You're probably right about everything."

Dana nodded as he left the room. But she hated that she didn't feel sure about anything right now. To make matters worse she was trapped in bed, her children were out making clay with a woman who her husband thought might be a kidnapper and meanwhile, her brother Jordan was involved in a murder case.

All she needed right now was for her younger brother, Clay, to show up.

Her babies moved. She splayed her fingers over them, whispered that she loved them and did her best not to cry.

Chapter Seven

Jordan hadn't been back to the cabin long when he heard a knock at his door. He put his unfinished sandwich in the small kitchenette refrigerator, then peeked out the window. He was in no mood for company.

"You've been holding out on me," Liza said when he finally opened the door.

He'd let her knock for a while, then had given up that she wasn't going to take the hint and leave him alone. He was in no mood after his run-in with Tessa and no longer sure about Tanner's death any more than he was Alex's.

"I beg your pardon?" he said.

"Tessa Ryerson Spring. You dated her at the same time Tanner was dating Brittany."

He sighed and stepped back to let Liza in, not wanting to discuss this on the cabin stoop. "I'd forgotten I dated her."

"Uh-huh." The deputy marshal came into the small cabin and looked around. "Why did you and Alex fight over her?"

Jordan shook his head and laughed. "I don't recall."

She smiled. "Try again. It sounds as if it was quite the fight. Didn't speak to each other for years. Does that refresh your memory?" She sat down on the end of his bed and crossed her legs, leaning back on her hands, her gaze on him.

"Make yourself comfortable," he said sarcastically.

"I thought this might take a while."

He sighed and pulled out a chair from the small table that constituted the dining room. He straddled it and leaned his arms on the back as he looked at her. The woman was like a badger burrowing into a hole.

"Fine. It isn't something I like to talk about but since you're determined… Shelby talked Tessa into breaking up with Alex and going out with me so we could double date with Tanner and Brittany."

"Tessa was a spy?"

He nodded.

"But it doesn't explain why you dated Tessa. Or does it?" She grinned. "Brittany. You wanted to be close to her. Wow, what a tangled web we weave."

"Happy? When I found out what Shelby had done, I told Tessa off." He shrugged.

"Which explains why you and Alex got into a fight over her how exactly?"

"I might have called her some names. Alex took offense. When I told him how far Tessa would go to do Shelby's dirty work, he took a swing at me. I swung back. We were in high school. Stuff like that happened."

"Alex had forgotten all about it when he called to talk to you about Tanner?"

Jordan shrugged. "I assume so."

Liza got to her feet and walked around the cabin for a moment. "You all talk about high school as if it was kid stuff." She let out a chuckle. "You forget. *I* went to high school."

"That doesn't surprise me," Jordan quipped.

"Then this probably won't, either. I let mean things happen to other students. No, worse than that, sometimes I was part of those things. I ran into one of the girls who was terrorized recently. She told me that she still has scars from the way she was treated."

He said nothing, afraid she'd been that girl. Liza would have been just different enough that he suspected she hadn't been in a group like Shelby's. He'd sensed a rebellious spirit just under her surface, a fire that the girls who followed Shelby didn't have.

She suddenly turned to face him, her expression angry and defiant. "Don't tell me that what happened in high school didn't matter. It mattered to Tanner and now I believe it has something to do with Alex Winslow's death, as well. What I'm trying to understand is what *happened*."

"You and me both," he said, feeling guilty because he'd been one of the popular kids. In his teens he hadn't given much thought to those who weren't. "If it helps, I saw Tessa today." He held up a hand before she could berate him for getting involved in her investigation. "*She* sought me out. I went to get a sandwich and she came in. She either followed me or had been looking for me."

"What did she want?"

"I don't know. Maybe just information about Alex's death. I thought at first Shelby had sent her. But then Shelby drove past and Tessa got all scared and left."

"What did you tell her?"

"She asked why anyone would want Alex dead. I said it could have something to do with him asking around about Tanner's death."

The deputy sheriff let out an unladylike curse.

"I wanted to see her reaction."

"And?"

"It spooked the hell out of her. She knows something. When I was talking to her I had a thought. If Tanner *did* kill himself, it would have had to be over something big. What if Shelby didn't have a miscarriage? What if she lied about that, maybe as a test to see if Tanner loved her, who knows?"

"What are you suggesting, that she was never pregnant?"

"No, that she aborted the baby," he said. "That she did it out of meanness to get back at him. To hurt him in a way that would haunt him to his grave."

Liza said nothing for a few moments. "You think that little of Shelby?"

He met her gaze and held it. "Tessa is her best friend. She knows the truth. I also think she's scared of that truth coming out."

"Wait, even if you're right and Shelby did do something to get back at Tanner, that wouldn't be something that she'd kill Alex to keep secret."

"Couldn't it? Shelby is all about getting what she wants, whatever it takes, and Tessa and her other minions have always followed her blindly."

"You don't think they'd draw the line when it came to out-and-out murder?" Liza demanded.

"Not if they had something to do with Tanner's death. What's another body if Alex was getting too close to the truth?"

Liza nodded. "So your graduating class from Big Sky was small, right?"

Jordan reached behind him to pick up the crumpled

piece of paper he'd left on the table. "This is the list of people who RSVP'd that they would be attending the reunion this weekend," he said, handing it to her. "I marked the other two girls who ran with Shelby in high school. Ashley and Whitney."

Liza considered the wrinkled-up paper in her hand, then looked at him quizzically.

"I had to dig it out of the trash before I flew out here. I wasn't planning to attend—until Alex called. Then I was curious about who was coming."

"Let me guess," Liza said. "You're planning on going to the reunion now?"

He smiled. "Not without a date. What do you say? Come on, this way you can get to see all the players in their natural habitat."

Liza actually seemed at a loss for words for a moment. "I feel like you're asking me to the prom."

"If you're expecting a corsage, a rented limo, champagne and a fancy hotel room afterwards…" He saw her expression and stopped. "You didn't go to prom?"

"I'm not wearing a prom dress," she said, ignoring his question.

"Just don't wear your silver star or your gun," he joked, hating that he'd been right. She was one of the girls who'd been tormented by girls like Shelby and Tessa.

LIZA STOOD IN FRONT OF HER closet. She hated to admit how few dresses she owned—and what she did have were old and out of style, though hardly worn. Worse, she hated that she cared what she wore to the reunion.

She'd been a tomboy, so dresses had never really appealed to her. Add to that her profession, she'd had little need of anything besides jeans and boots.

"I don't know what I'm going to wear," she said when Dana answered the phone. "I know it doesn't matter. It's not like it's a date."

"No, going out with a suspect probably couldn't be called a date," her boss's wife agreed with a chuckle. "Come over. You're welcome to dig through my closet. I'll call Hilde. She's more girlie than either of us. She'll help."

"Thanks," Liza said, relieved. She definitely needed help.

"How is the investigation going?" Dana asked.

Liza knew Dana must be bored to tears now that she was being forced to stay in bed. "Slowly." She didn't want to admit that it brought up a lot of high school memories, ones she thought she'd left behind when she'd graduated.

"And Jordan?" Dana asked.

She didn't know how to answer that. "He's fine. Actually, I get the feeling he's changed. Don't worry," she said quickly. "If he hasn't, I'll be the first to know. He's still a suspect."

"But you don't think he killed Alex Winslow."

"No. I think he really did come back to find out what happened to his friend Tanner. It's looking like he had reason to be concerned."

Dana was silent for a moment. "Tell him to stop by, if he wants to."

"I will. I'll drop by later this afternoon for the clothing search." In the meantime, she thought, closing her closet door, she wanted to pay Tessa Ryerson Spring a visit.

DANA COULDN'T HELP THINKING of Jordan and half wishing she hadn't told Liza to have him stop by. Feeling the babies kick, she willed herself not to worry about Stacy or her brother. Instead, she put in a quick call to Hilde, who, of course, was delighted to help with Liza's clothing dilemma.

"I'll gather up some dresses and bring them over later," her best friend said. "Can I bring you anything?"

"Maybe some needlepoint from the store?" Dana suggested, cringing since the mere thought had always given her hives.

"Oh, girl, you really are bored to tears!" She laughed as she hung up.

After she'd found her mother's will and got to go back to ranching, Dana had become a silent partner in Needles and Pins, the small sewing shop she and Hilde had started in Meadow Village. She'd never been the one who sewed. That had been Hilde. But Dana had always loved working with her best friend in the shop.

She missed it sometimes. Not that she and the kids didn't often stop in to visit. Mary and Hank loved all the colorful bolts of fabric and Hilde always had some fun craft for them to do.

"Look what we made, Mommy!" Mary and Hank cried in unison now as they came running into the bedroom. They held up the clay figures, and Dana praised them for their imagination and their choice of multiple bright colors.

Behind them, Stacy stood in the doorway looking on with what appeared to be contentment. Dana had been watching her sister all day. She hated letting Hud's suspicions cloud her forgiving thoughts about Stacy. She'd missed having a sister all these years. Not that she and Stacy had been close like some sisters. There were no tea parties, doll playing or dressing up for pretend weddings.

Stacy had done all those things, but Dana had been an outside kid. She loved riding her horse, climbing trees, building forts. Two years older, Stacy had turned up her nose at most things Dana thought were fun and vice versa.

"Okay, let's clean up our mess," her sister told the kids. "I think that's your daddy who just drove up."

As they scampered out of the room, leaving a couple clay figures beside her bed to keep her company, Dana waited expectantly for Hud. She knew where he'd gone and what he'd been up to—running a check on her sister. A part of her feared what he might have discovered.

She listened. The moment he came in the house, Mary and Hank were all over him. He played with them for a moment, and, like her, praised everything they'd made before coming into the bedroom. When he closed the door, she knew the news wasn't going to be good.

LIZA COULDN'T SHAKE the feeling that Jordan was right about the two deaths being connected. While anxious to talk to Tessa Ryerson Spring, she went to the office and pulled out the Tanner Cole investigation file. There wasn't much in it since the coroner had ruled the death a suicide.

The incident had happened back up the North Fork where the victim had been staying in a cabin. His body had been found hanging from a tree limb in sight of the cabin, a rope noose around the victim's neck. There was evidence of a log stump having been dragged over under the limb of the tree. When the body was found, the stump was on its side, a good foot from the dead man's dangling boots. Cause of death was strangulation.

The victim was found by Jordan Cardwell, who'd gone looking for Tanner when he hadn't shown up for school.

Attached were a half dozen black-and-white photographs taken at the scene. She flipped through them, noticing that the tree where Tanner was found hanging was next to a fire ring. She could see that there were dozens of footprints around the scene, no doubt because the area had been used for a party. Other stumps had been dragged up around the campfire area. Numerous discarded beer cans could be seen charred black in the firepit.

As she started to put the file back, something caught her eye. The investigating officer had been Brick Savage—Hud's father.

HUD SMILED SHEEPISHLY at his wife after closing the door. She was watching him expectantly. He wished she didn't know him so well sometimes. Walking over to the bed, he bent down and, touching her cheek, kissed her. "You get more beautiful every day."

She swatted his hand playfully as he drew back. "If you think you can charm me—"

He laughed as she moved over to let him sit on the edge of the bed next to her. "Just speaking the truth." She *was* beautiful. The pregnancy had put a glow in her cheeks and her eyes. Not that she wasn't a stunner anytime. Dana had always smelled of summer, an indefinable scent that filled his heart like helium. He counted his blessings every day he woke up next to her.

"Okay, charmer, let's hear it," she said. "With you being so sweet, I'm guessing it's bad news."

He shook his head. "Am I that transparent?"

"Hud," she said impatiently.

"I didn't find out much. There wasn't much to find out. Apparently, she doesn't have credit cards or even a checking account."

"She's in the process of moving and not having credit cards is a good thing."

He sighed, seeing that she was determined to think the best. But then, that was Dana. But with her family, their history proved out that he definitely had reason to be suspicious. He knew she wanted to believe that Stacy had changed. He did, too. He was just a whole lot more skeptical than Dana.

"A tiger doesn't change its spots," he said.

"Isn't it 'a zebra doesn't change its stripes' and what does that even mean?" she demanded.

"I had a look in her car last night after everyone went to bed. If she's moving to Great Falls, she sure didn't pack much." He held up his hand. "I know. She apparently doesn't have any money. But she gets the check from the ranch profits."

"You know that isn't enough to live on."

"Well, you'd think she would have had a job for the past six years."

"Stacy didn't go to college so more than likely she can't make much more than minimum wage."

He shook his head. "I could find no employment in her past."

"So she worked off the books somewhere. Or maybe the baby's father has been taking care of her and now she can't work because she has a baby to raise."

Yeah, Hud thought. That's what had Dana so desperate to believe Stacy had changed. That baby. Ella was cute as a bug's ear. No doubt about that. Just the thought of Stacy raising the child, though, terrified him.

"So that's all you found," Dana said.

He nodded. "No warrants or outstanding violations." No missing kids on Amber Alert who matched either the name Katie—or Ella's description.

"So there is nothing to worry about."

"Right." He just wished he could shake his uneasy feeling.

"And don't you go interrogating her," Dana said. "Give her the benefit of the doubt. She is in absolute awe of that baby. She couldn't be prouder of Ella. It's the first time I've seen my sister like this."

He nodded, not wanting to argue with her. He needed to keep Dana in this bed for their twins' sake. Placing a hand on her stomach, he felt their babies move. It had a calming affect on him. Just as being here with his family did.

But in the other room he could hear Stacy with the kids. Something wasn't right with her story. Call it his marshal intuition. But Stacy wasn't telling them the truth. And as much as he hated to think it, whatever she was lying about, it had something to do with that precious baby.

TESSA RYERSON SPRING didn't answer her phone so Liza drove over to the house. Getting out of the patrol SUV, she walked past the garage, noting that at least one vehicle was inside, before she rang the doorbell.

She had to ring it four times and knock hard before Tessa appeared. She'd wrapped a towel around her head and pulled a robe on, no doubt hoping Liza would think she'd been in the shower.

"I'm sorry," she said, looking more than a little flustered. "Have you been standing here long?"

Long enough. "Mind if I come in for a moment? Or you can come down to the office? Which works better for you?"

"Actually, I was just…" Tessa gave up and said, "I suppose I have a few minutes." She stepped aside to let Liza in. "I should make some coffee."

"No, thanks. Why don't we sit down for a minute." She could tell that Tessa wanted something to occupy herself. Jordan was right about one thing. Tessa was nervous and clearly afraid.

"This won't take long," Liza assured her.

The woman finally perched on the edge of the couch. Liza took a chair across from her. Like many of the residences at Big Sky, the decor was made to look like the Old West from the leather furniture to the antler lamps. The floor was hardwood, the rugs Native American, the fireplace local granite.

Tessa straightened the hem of her robe to cover whatever she was wearing beneath it, then fiddled with the sash.

"I'm here about Alex Winslow's death."

"Oh?" Her smile was tentative. "Why would you want to talk to *me?*"

"You were a friend of his in high school."

"Yes, but that was twenty years ago."

"But you talked to him recently. The calls were on his cell phone," Liza said.

Tessa's eyes widened with alarm. Her hand went to her forehead as if suddenly struck with a migraine.

Clearly she hadn't expected anyone to know about the calls.

"I'm curious what you talked about," Liza said.

After a moment the woman pulled herself together. "I'm sorry. I'm just upset. I heard he was murdered?"

"So what did you talk about?"

"The reunion. Shelby must have told him to call me. I'm in charge of the picnic on Sunday. It's going to be at the top of the gondola. Weather permitting, of course." Her smile was weak, nervous. She worked at the robe sash with her fingers, toying with the edges.

"You and Alex dated in high school."

She nodded. "For a short while."

"But you were close?"

"I'm not sure what you mean."

"I mean Alex trusted you. He would have confided in you."

"I don't know what you're asking."

"He would have told you if he had some reason to suspect that Tanner Cole didn't kill himself." The statement had the effect Liza had hoped for.

Fear shone in the woman's eyes. Her hand went to her throat. Jordan was right. She knew *something*.

"Had you ever been up to the cabin where Tanner was staying that spring before high school graduation?" Liza asked.

"I might have."

"With Alex?"

"Maybe. I really can't remember."

"Do you knit?" Liza asked.

"What?"

"I wondered if you knitted because this case started like a loose thread in a sweater. At first it was just a small problem, but once it started unraveling…" She shook her head. "Alex started it unraveling. Now it's going to come apart. No doubt about it."

Tessa managed a smile. "That's an odd simile."

"Metaphor," Liza said. "It's a metaphor for murder. Alex was just the beginning. As this unravels, more people are going to die. Because even though you believe you can keep this secret, whoever killed Alex is afraid you can't. You see how this works? You just can't trust each other anymore and when push comes to shove…"

"I'm sorry, deputy," Tessa said, getting to her feet. "I have no idea what you're talking about and I'm running late for an appointment. She held her head in a regal manner. Liza got a glimpse of the girl Tessa had been when she and Shelby and the others had been on the pinnacle of popularity and thought nothing could bring them down. But as they all seemed fond of saying, "that was high school." This was real life.

"Think about it, Tessa. If they think you're the weak link, they'll attack you like rabid dogs." Liza rose. "I'll see myself out."

Chapter Eight

Jordan hadn't seen his father since the last time he was in Montana. They talked once in a while by phone, but they really didn't have much to say to each other.

For a long time Jordan blamed his mother for the divorce, believing she cared more about the ranch than she did her husband. There was probably some truth in that. But the divorce wasn't all her fault. She hadn't driven his father away. Angus Cardwell was more than capable of doing that himself.

He found his father at Angus's favorite watering hole, the Corral, down the canyon from Big Sky. Angus had been one handsome cowboy in his day. It was easy to see even now why Mary Justice had fallen in love with him.

Unfortunately, Jordan's mother had loved ranching and her husband had loved bars and booze. The two hadn't mixed well. Angus had taken the healthy settlement Mary had offered him and had left amicably enough. He'd made the money last by working an odd job here and there, including cash he and his brother made playing in a Country-Western band.

Most of the time though, Angus could be found on a

bar stool—just as he was now. And most of the time his brother Harlan would be with him—just as he was now.

"Well, look what the cat dragged in," Angus said as Jordan made his way down the bar toward them. Like all out-of-the-way Montana bars, everyone had looked up to see who'd come through the door. Angus and Harlan were no exceptions.

"Hey, Bob," his father called to the owner as he slid off his stool to shake Jordan's hand and pound him on the back. "You remember my eldest."

Bob nodded, said hello and dropped a bar napkin in front of an empty stool next to Angus. Uncle Harlan nodded his hello and Angus patted the stool next to him and said, "What would you like to drink, son?"

Jordan wasn't in the mood for a drink, but he knew better than to say so. Angus took it personally when anyone wouldn't drink with him—especially his son. "I'll take a beer. Whatever's on tap."

Bob poured him a cold one and set it on the napkin, taking the money out of the twenty Angus had beside his own beer.

"What are you doing in Montana?" Uncle Harlan asked.

"I was just asking myself that same thing," Jordan said and took a sip of his beer. He could feel his father's gaze on him. News traveled fast in the canyon. Angus and Harlan would have heard about the shooting night before last.

He braced himself for their questions. To his surprise, that wasn't the first thing his father wanted to know.

"Been to see your sister yet?" Angus asked.

"Not yet. I wasn't sure Dana would want to see me."

"You know better than that." He took a drink of his beer. "That is, unless you're going to try to hit her up for money. No one will want to see you in that case."

Jordan shook his head. "I'm not here looking for money."

"In that case," his father said with a laugh, "you can buy the next round."

Two beers later Jordan asked his father if he remembered when Tanner Cole died.

Angus nodded solemnly. "He hung himself up by that construction site. I remember he was staying up there because there'd been some vandalism."

"There'd been some before Tanner moved into the cabin?" Jordan asked in surprise.

Angus nodded. "Couldn't prove who did it, but Malcolm Iverson was pretty sure it was his competitor, Harris Lancaster, trying to put him out of business. So he hired the kid to keep an eye on things."

Jordan hadn't known about the earlier vandalism or that Iverson had suspected Harris Lancaster.

"Malcolm probably couldn't have survived financially the way things were going even if his equipment hadn't been vandalized a second time," Uncle Harlan said. "Your friend must have taken it hard, though, since everyone blamed it for forcing Iverson into bankruptcy. Apparently, he'd let his equipment insurance lapse."

"How did I never hear this?" Jordan said.

"You were a senior in high school," his father said with a laugh. "You had your nose up some girl's skirt. You were lucky you even graduated."

"Tanner never said anything about this," he said more to himself than to his father and uncle.

Angus tipped his beer up, took a swallow, then turned his gaze on his son. "You can't blame yourself. Malcolm had no business hiring a kid to watch over his equipment. I'm just sorry you had to be the one to find your friend like that."

Jordan nodded, remembering the day he'd gone up to the construction site looking for Tanner. He'd been worried about him since it wasn't like Tanner to miss school.

He'd never forget parking and walking up the road to find the front door of the cabin open. He'd called Tanner's name and gotten no answer and yet, his friend's pickup had been sitting next to the cabin.

One glance and he'd seen that it was empty. He'd heard the creaking sound and at first thought it was a tree limb scraping against another limb.

It wasn't until he turned toward the fire pit where the party had been held the night of the vandalism that he saw the shadow. A breeze had stirred the pines, making the shadow flicker over the dead campfire. He'd called Tanner's name again, then with a sinking feeling he'd followed the creaking sound until he saw what was casting the long shadow over the fire ring.

He would never forget the sight of his best friend hanging from the tree limb.

Jordan took a drink of his beer, cleared his throat and said, "I never believed that Tanner killed himself. I knew he blamed himself for the vandalism because of the party up there that night, but now with Alex murdered… I have to find out what really happened."

"If I were you, I'd stay out of it," Angus said, looking worried. "Two of your friends are dead. Whatever's going on, you might be next."

LIZA HAD TO ADMIT IT. She was having fun. She and Dana had hit it off from the first time they'd met and Hilde was a whole lot of fun.

"Oh, you have to try this one," Hilde said as she pulled a black-and-white polka-dot dress from the huge pile she'd brought. "It's one of my favorites."

They'd been laughing and joking as Liza tried on one dress after another. Hilde had kidded Dana after exploring her closet and deeming it probably worse than Liza's.

"You cowgirls," Hilde said. "Jeans, jeans, jeans. Don't you ever just want to show off your legs?"

"No," Liza and Dana had said in unison.

The polka-dot dress was cute and it fit Liza perfectly. "Do you think it's *too* cute? Maybe it's not dressy enough," Liza asked.

"Come on, this is Montana, no one dresses up," Dana said.

Hilde rolled her eyes. "Sweetie, this is Big Sky and all the women will be dressed to the nines. The men will be wearing jeans, boots and Western sports jackets, but for these women, this is a chance to pull out all those expensive clothes, bags and high heels they're just dying to show off."

"Then I'm wearing this," Liza said, studying her reflection in the mirror. She loved the black-and-white polka-dot dress. "This is as dressy as this cowgirl is going to get."

Dana laughed. "Good for you."

As Liza changed back into her jeans, boots and uniform shirt, Dana said, "So have you seen my brother?"

She shook her head. "Not since earlier. I haven't had a chance to talk to him, either."

"He is still a suspect, right?" Hilde asked, sounding worried.

Liza realized that her two friends were worried about her being taken in by Jordan. She had to smile, warmed by their concern.

"I hope I don't have to remind you that he was best friends with both Tanner and Alex and now they're both dead," Hilde said. "I grew up around Jordan. He always had a temper." She shot a look at Dana, who nodded, though with obvious regret.

"People change," Liza said, instantly regretting coming to Jordan's defense. She saw Hilde and Dana exchange a look. *"What?"*

"It's Stacy. I think *she's* changed," Dana said.

"You *hope* she's changed," Hilde corrected.

"Hud told me he was doing some checking into her past," Liza said. "I assume he didn't find anything."

"That's just it, he found nothing and that has him even more worried," Dana said. "Him and his marshal intuition."

Liza laughed. "Don't be joking around about our intuition." She'd been a green deputy six years ago, but Hud had taken her under his wing after seeing what he called an instinct for the job. Now he trusted her to handle this investigation and that meant everything to her.

The three women visited for a while longer, then Liza said she had to get moving. "The cocktail party and dinner is tonight. I've studied up on the players. Jordan had a list of those attending. Surprisingly, or maybe not, all eight of the Big Sky senior graduates will be up at Mountain Village tonight. Everyone but Alex and Tanner, that is." It was a small class twenty years ago. Although they attended high school down in Bozeman, they wanted their own reunion up here. Only in the past few years had Big Sky gotten its own high school.

"Just be careful," Dana said. "I know a few of those women." She pretended to shudder. "They're vicious."

"I don't think they're that bad," Hilde said. "I work out at Yogamotion. They're nice to me."

This time Dana and Liza exchanged a look. Hilde was petite, blonde and lithe. She would fit right in.

Dana reached for Liza's hand and squeezed it. "Just don't forget that one of them could be a killer."

JORDAN HAD SPENT THE REST of the afternoon writing down everything he could remember about his senior year of high school, especially what might pertain to Tanner and Alex.

The trip down memory lane had exhausted him. When he glanced at his watch, he'd been shocked to see how late it was. He quickly showered and changed and drove over to pick up his date.

What surprised him was the frisson of excitement he felt as he rang Liza's bell. He realized with a start that he hadn't been on a real date in years. Since his divorce he'd stayed clear of women.

When he'd left the canyon, he'd shed the cowboy side of him like an old snakeskin. He'd wanted bright lights and big city. He'd wanted sophistication. He'd kicked the Montana ranch dust off his boots and hadn't looked back.

That was how he'd ended up married to Jill. He'd been flattered that a model would even give him a second look. She'd been thrilled that he came from Montana ranch stock, saying she was bored with New York City–type men.

What he hadn't realized was that Jill thought he had money. She'd thought the ranch was the size of Ted Turner's apparently and couldn't wait to get her hands on the funds it would bring in once it sold.

He'd gotten caught up in trying to make her happy, even though she'd quit modeling the moment they were married and spent her days spending more money than he could make on Wall Street.

Now he could admit that he had become obsessed with keeping her. Although he hadn't acknowledged it to himself back then, he'd known that if he ran out of money, Jill would run out on him.

And she had—just as Dana had predicted. He hadn't wanted to hear it six years ago. Hell, he didn't like to think about it even now. The truth hurt. He'd fought back, of course, driving an even wider wedge between himself and his younger sister.

When Dana had discovered their mother's new will in that damned cookbook at the ranch house, Jill had realized there would be no ranch sale, no gold at the end of the rainbow, and she'd split. In truth, she'd already had some New York male model lined up long before that.

It had been some hard knocks, but he felt as if they had maybe knocked some sense into him. He saw things clearer than he had before. Mary Justice Cardwell had tried to instill values in her children. He'd rejected most of them, but they were still at his core, he thought as he rang Liza Turner's doorbell again.

When the door opened, he was taken completely off guard by the woman standing there. Liza took his breath away. She was wearing a black-and-white polka-dot dress that accentuated curves he'd had no idea were beneath her uniform. Her beautiful long curly hair had been pulled up, wisps of curls framing her face and she smelled heavenly.

"Wow, you look killer," he said when he caught his breath.

"So to speak," she said, sounding embarrassed as she quickly stuffed her gun into her purse. "My feet already hurt in these shoes."

He smiled at her. "You can kick them off the minute we hit the dance floor."

"Dance floor?" she asked, cocking an eyebrow.

"Didn't I mention I do one hell of a two-step?"

She took him in, her gaze pausing on his cowboy boots.

"Dana had a box of my clothes dropped off at the cabin," he said, feeling sheepish. It was so like Dana to be thoughtful. He'd found the boots as well as a couple of dress Western shirts and a Western-cut sports coat. He'd been surprised when everything still fit.

"You are a man of many surprises," she said, sounding almost as if she meant it.

He laughed. "You haven't seen anything yet." As he walked her to his rental SUV, he breathed in her scent, thinking he couldn't wait to get this woman in his arms on the dance floor.

DANA SUCKED ON HER BLEEDING finger. Needlepoint wasn't for her, she decided after jabbing herself another time. She surveyed her stitches and cringed. As Stacy came into the bedroom, she tossed the needlepoint aside, glad for an interruption.

Earlier, Mary and Hank had come in and colored

with her before their naps. She missed holding them on her lap, missed even more riding horses with them around the corral. All these beautiful fall days felt wasted lying in bed. But Hud had promised to take both kids out tomorrow.

As Stacy came over to the side of her bed, Dana saw that her sister had the cookbook open to their mother's double chocolate brownies.

"Is it all right if I make these?" Stacy asked.

They were Hud's favorite. That's why Mary Justice Cardwell had tucked her new will in her old, worn and faded cookbook next to the recipe. She'd wanted Dana not only to have the ranch—but the man she loved beside her.

"Sure. Hud would like that," Dana said, disappointed she couldn't even do something as simple as bake a pan of brownies for her husband.

"Mother used to make them for Dad, remember? Do you ever see him?"

"On occasion. Usually a holiday. He and Uncle Harlan keep pretty busy with their band." And their drinking, but she didn't say that.

Stacy nodded. "I might see them while I'm here. Maybe tomorrow if you don't mind me leaving for a little while in the morning?"

"Stacy, you don't need to ask. Of course you can go. Hud will be here."

"I suppose I know where I'll find Dad. Would you mind keeping Ella? I won't go until I put her down for her morning nap. I don't want to take her to a bar."

"I would be happy to watch her. You can bring her in here for her nap. She'll be fine while you're gone."

Stacy smiled, tears in her eyes, and gave Dana an

impulsive though awkward hug. "I've missed you so much."

"I've missed you, too."

Her sister drew back, looking embarrassed, grabbed the cookbook and left. In the other room, Hud was playing fort with the kids. She could see a corner of the couch and chairs pulled into the middle of the room and covered with spare blankets.

Hud caught her eye. He smiled and shrugged as if to say, maybe she was right about her sister. Dana sure hoped so.

LIZA BRACED HERSELF AS JORDAN ushered her into the lodge at Mountain Village for the Friday-night dinner and dance. Tomorrow there would be a tour of Big Sky and a free afternoon, with the final picnic Sunday.

A room had been prepared for the reunion party that impressed her more than she wanted to admit. A DJ played music under a starry decor of silver and white. The lights had been turned low, forming pockets of darkness. Candles flickered at white-clothed tables arranged in a circle around the small shining dance floor.

A few couples were dancing. Most were visiting, either standing next to the bar or already seated at the cocktail tables.

"Hilde was right," Liza whispered. "I *am* underdressed." The women were dressed in fancy gowns and expensive accessories. The men wore jeans and boots and Western sports jackets, looking much like Jordan.

"You look beautiful, the prettiest woman here," Jordan said, putting his arm around her protectively.

She grinned over at him. "You really can be charming when you want to, Mr. Cardwell."

"Don't tell Hud," he said. "I've spent years cultivating his bad opinion of me. I'd hate to ruin it with just one night with you." He put his hand on her waist. "Let's dance." He drew her out on the dance floor and pulled her close. She began to move to the slow song, too aware of her dance partner and his warm hand on her back.

Jordan *was* full of surprises. He was light on his feet, more athletic than she'd thought and a wonderful dancer. He held her close, the two of them moving as one, and she lost herself in the music and him as she rested her cheek against his shoulder. He smelled wonderful and she felt safe and protected in his arms. The latter surprised her.

The night took on a magical feel and for the length of several Country-Western songs, she forgot why she and Jordan were here. She also forgot that he was a murder suspect.

When the song ended, she found herself looking at him as if seeing him for the first time. He appeared completely at home in his Western clothes. They suited him and she told him so.

He smiled at that. "I thought I'd dusted the cowboy dirt off me when I left here. My mother used to say this land and life were a part of me that I could never shed." He quickly changed the subject as if he hadn't meant to tell her those things. "Looks like everyone is here except for Tessa, Alex and Tanner. That's the nice thing about having a small graduating class. They're fairly easy to keep track of. Shall we get a drink?"

They'd done just that by the end of the next song when Shelby took the stage. She gave a short speech, updating anyone who didn't know about the members of the class, announced who had come the farthest, who had changed the most, who had the most kids.

"I thought we should have a few minutes of silence for Alex," she said at the end. "Since he can't be with us tonight."

Liza spotted Tessa, who'd apparently just arrived. There was chatter about the murder around the tables, then everyone grew silent. It seemed to stretch on too long. Liza found herself looking around the room at the graduates.

She quickly picked out the main players Jordan had told her about. Shelby and her husband, contractor Wyatt Iverson; Tessa, who'd come alone; Whitney Fraser and husband and local business owner, Von; and Ashley Henderson and husband, Paul, had all congregated to one area of the room. Ashley and her husband and Whitney and hers appeared to be cut from the same cloth as Shelby and Wyatt. Brittany Peterson and husband Lee were visiting at a table of former students who were no longer Big Sky residents.

As Liza took them all in, she knew that what she was really looking for was a killer.

Wyatt Iverson was as handsome and put-together as his wife, Shelby. Liza waited until he went to the bar alone before she joined him.

"Wyatt Iverson? I don't think we've met. I'm Liza Turner—"

"Deputy marshal in charge of the Alex Winslow case," he said with a wide smile. "I know. I checked. I wanted to make sure someone capable was on the case. I heard great things about you."

"Thank you." She recalled a rumor going around that Wyatt was considering getting into national politics.

Right now he served on a variety of boards as well as on the local commission. Wyatt was handsome and a smooth talker, a born politician and clearly a man with a driving ambition. He'd brought his father's business back from bankruptcy and made a name for himself, not to mention a whole lot of money apparently.

Shelby joined them, taking her husband's arm and announcing that dinner was being served in the dining room. "Everyone bring your drinks and follow me!" Ashley and Whitney fell into line and trailed after Shelby, just as Tessa did, but according to Jordan they'd been doing that for years.

To no one's surprise, Shelby had distributed place cards around a long table. Liza was surprised to see that she and Jordan were near the center, with Tessa and Brittany and her husband, Lee, at one end and Shelby's inner circle at the other.

She noticed that Tessa seemed surprised—and upset—when she found herself at the far end of the table. Clearly Tessa had done something Shelby hadn't liked. Either that or Shelby was sending her friend a message. If Shelby had anything to do with Alex's murder and Tessa knew about it, Liza feared that Tessa might get more than banished at the reunion dinner table. Whatever had Shelby upset with her could get Tessa killed just as it had Alex.

Chapter Nine

Jordan could have wrung Shelby's neck even before dinner was served. They'd all just sat down when Shelby insisted everyone go around the table and introduce their dates and spouses before dinner was served.

When it came Jordan's turn, he squeezed Liza's hand and said, "This is my date, Liza Turner."

"Oh, come on, Jordan," Shelby said. "Liza Turner is our local deputy marshal and the woman in charge of investigating Alex's murder." She smiled as she said it, but Jordan couldn't miss the hard glint in her eyes. "So, Deputy, tell us how the case is going."

"It's under investigation, that's all I can tell you," Liza said.

Shelby pretended to pout, making Jordan grit his teeth. "Oh, we were hoping as Alex's friends we could get inside information."

Jordan just bet she was. Fortunately, the staff served dinner and the conversations turned to other things.

"How have you been?" Brittany asked him. She was still as strikingly beautiful as she'd been in high school, but now there was a contentment about her.

"Good. You look happy," he said, glad for her.

"My life is as crazy as ever with three small ones

running around and…" She grinned. "Another one on the way. Surprise!"

"Congratulations," Jordan said, meaning it. She didn't seem in the least bit upset to be seated away from Shelby and her other classmates. Unlike Tessa, who hadn't said a word or hardly looked up since sitting down.

Everyone offered their congratulations to Brittany, including Shelby, who seemed to have her ears trained on their end of the table.

"How many does this make now?" she asked.

"Four, Shelby," Brittany said, smiling although Jordan could tell Shelby irritated her as much as she did him.

Shelby pretended shock. "I think you get the award for most children and also our Look Who's Pregnant! Award."

Jordan glanced over at Liza. He knew she was taking all of this in. Like him, he was sure she'd noticed the way Tessa had been acting since they'd sat down. Also, Tessa had been hitting the booze hard every time she could get the cocktail waitress's attention.

Jordan couldn't have been happier when dessert was finally served. Shelby had been running the dinner as if it was a board meeting. He noticed that, like Tessa, Shelby had been throwing down drinks. Just the sound of her voice irritated him. He was reminded why he hadn't wanted to come to his reunion.

"Jordan, what was the name of your wife, the one who was the model?" Shelby asked loudly from the other end of the table.

He didn't want to talk about his marriage or his divorce. But he knew Shelby wasn't going to let it go.

"Jill Ames. She was my *only* wife, Shelby," he said and felt Liza's calming hand on his thigh.

"Jill Ames is *gorgeous*. What were you thinking letting her get away?" Shelby said and laughed. She gave Liza a sympathetic look. "Jill Ames would be a hard act to follow."

"Shelby, you might want to back off on the drinks," Brittany said, throwing down her napkin as she shoved to her feet. "Your claws are coming out." She shot Jordan and Liza an apologetic look and excused herself before heading for the ladies' room. Shelby glared after her for a moment, then followed her.

LIZA WAITED UNTIL SHELBY disappeared down the hallway before she, too, excused herself. She was within ten feet of the ladies' room door when she heard their raised voices. She slowed, checked to make sure there was no one behind her, before she stepped to the door and eased it open a few inches. She could see the two reflected in the bathroom mirrors, but neither could see her.

"How dare you try to embarrass me," Shelby screeched into Brittany's face.

"Embarrass *you?* Seriously, Shelby?" Brittany started to turn away from her.

Shelby grabbed her arm. "Don't you turn your back on me."

"Touch me again and I'll deck you," Brittany said as she jerked free of the woman's hold. "I don't do yoga every day like you, but I do haul around three kids so I'm betting I'm a lot stronger and tougher than you are. I'm also not afraid of you anymore."

"Well, you should be."

"Are you threatening me?" Brittany demanded as

she advanced on her. "This isn't high school, Shelby. Your reign is over." She turned and went into a stall.

Shelby stood as if frozen on the spot, her face white with fury as Liza stepped into the ladies' room. Seeing the deputy marshal, Shelby quickly spun around and twisted the handle on the faucet, hiding her face as she washed her hands.

Liza went into the first stall. She heard Brittany flush, exit the next stall and go to the washbasin. Through the sound of running water, she heard Shelby hiss something.

"Whatever, Shelby." Brittany left, but a moment later someone else came in.

"Aren't you talking to me? What's going on?" Tessa whined, sounding like a child. "Are you mad at me? I don't understand. I haven't done *anything*."

She was sure Shelby was probably trying to signal that they weren't alone, but Tessa was clearly upset and apparently not paying attention.

"I told you I wouldn't say anything. You know you can trust me. So why are you—"

"Tessa, this really isn't the place," Shelby snapped.

"But all evening you've—"

Liza had no choice but to flush. As she opened the stall door, both Tessa and Shelby glanced in her direction. "Ladies," she said as she moved to the sinks and turned on the water.

"I could use some fresh air," Shelby said. "Come outside with me for a minute." She smiled as she took Tessa's arm and practically dragged her out of the bathroom.

Liza washed her hands, dried them and then stepped out. She could see Shelby and Tessa on the large deck in what was obviously a heated discussion. She watched them for a moment, wishing she could hear their conversation, but having no way to do that went back to the table and Jordan.

"Everything okay?" he asked quietly.

She smiled at him. "Great."

"I love your dress," Brittany said.

Liza laughed. "That's right. You like polka dots. I remember your apron." Liza liked Brittany. She could see why Jordan had had a crush on her in high school. Probably still did.

With dinner over, everyone began to wander away from the table and back into the first room where the music was again playing.

Liza pulled Jordan aside and told him what she'd overheard.

"So basically you just wanted to let me know I was right about Tessa," Jordan said, grinning.

"Apparently, you can be right once in a while, yes." She smiled back at him, realizing he was flirting with her again and she didn't mind it.

A few moments later Shelby came back in from the deck. She put her game face on again and breezed by them, already dancing to the music before she reached the dance floor. But she didn't fool Liza. Shelby was trying hard to hide whatever was really going on with her and Tessa.

"I'm going to talk to Tessa," Liza said. "Save me a dance."

As Jordan left the dining room and joined the others, he spotted Shelby talking to her other two cohorts. Ashley and Whitney could have been sisters. They were both brunettes, both shapely, both pretty—at least from a distance. He knew his perception of them had been poisoned a long time ago.

He liked to think all of them had changed, himself included. But he could tell by the way Ashley and Whitney were listening to Shelby that they still followed her as blindly as they had in high school. It made him sad. Brittany had grown up, made a life for herself and seen through Shelby. But apparently Brittany was the only one who'd made the break from Shelby's control.

"Jordan, do you have a minute?"

He turned to find Paul Henderson, Ashley's husband. Paul had been two years ahead of them in school. "Sure," he said as Paul motioned to the empty lobby of the lodge.

"I hope I'm not speaking out of school here," Paul said. "But there's a rumor going around that Alex was asking about Tanner before he was…killed. I figured if you really were with him at the falls, then he must have talked to you."

"We didn't get a chance to talk," Jordan said, wondering if Paul had any information or if he was just fishing.

"Oh." He looked crestfallen.

"*You* talked to him?"

Paul nodded and met Jordan's gaze. "I wasn't sure if I should tell the deputy marshal."

"What did Alex tell you?"

He hesitated for a moment, then said, "Alex asked me if I remembered the party Tanner had that night at the cabin, the night the equipment was vandalized?"

Jordan nodded. He vaguely remembered the party. He'd drunk too much and, after his fight with Tessa, had left early with some girl from Bozeman who he couldn't even remember. "Were you there?"

"No. I was grounded from the past weekend. He was asking if I knew where Shelby was that night."

"Shelby?"

"He wanted to know if Ashley had been with her."

"And was she?"

"That's just it. I told Alex that I thought she was because she called a little after two in the morning. She'd been drinking. We argued and I hung up. The next day when I asked her where she'd been the night before, she swore she didn't go to the party. But Alex said something about some photos from the party that night that proved not only were Ashley and Whitney there, but Shelby and Tessa were, too."

"Why was he interested in photos of the party?" Jordan asked.

Paul shrugged. "That's just it. I can't imagine what some photographs of a high school kegger twenty years ago could have to do with anything. That's why I haven't said anything to the deputy marshal."

"Did you ask Ashley about them?"

"She still swears she wasn't at the party that night, but…" He looked away for a moment. "I'd like to see those photos. Alex seemed to think there was something in them that could explain why Tanner is dead."

"I'll mention it to the deputy marshal," Jordan said. "She might want to talk to you."

Paul looked relieved. "I didn't know if I should say anything, but I'm glad I did. Okay, back to the party huh?" He didn't look as if he was enjoying the reunion any more than Jordan had enjoyed dinner.

The only thing that kept Jordan from calling it quits was the thought of another dance with Liza.

TESSA STOOD AT THE DECK railing, her back to the lodge. She looked cold and miserable and from the redness around her eyes, she'd been crying.

Liza joined her at the railing. "Shelby's trying to bring you back under control, you know."

Tessa glanced over at her and let out a laugh. "I'd pretend I didn't know what you were talking about, but what would be the use?"

"Talk to me, Tessa. Tell me what Shelby is so terrified I'll find out?"

Tessa hugged herself and looked away. A breeze whispered in the nearby pines. Earlier it had been warm. Now though, the air had cooled. It carried the promise of winter. Closer, Liza could hear the muted music from inside the lodge. The party was resuming. She was betting that Shelby wouldn't leave Tessa out here long. If Liza didn't get the truth out of her quickly—

A door opened behind them. "Tessa?" Whitney called from the open doorway. "Shelby needs your help with the awards."

"I'll be right there," she said over her shoulder and started to turn toward the lodge.

"Tessa," Liza said, feeling her chance slipping through her fingers. She was genuinely afraid for Tessa. For some reason, the woman had been cut from the herd. Liza feared for the woman's life.

"Let me think about things. Maybe I'll stop by your office Monday."

Liza nodded. The one thing she'd learned was when to back off. "I can help you."

Tessa laughed at that and looked toward the lodge. "I'm not sure anyone can help me," she said and pushed off the railing to go back inside.

Liza bit down on her frustration. Tessa needed her best friend's approval. But surely she was tired of playing Shelby's game.

Telling herself this night hadn't been a total waste, Liza waited for a few moments before going back inside. The moment she saw Jordan, she thought, no, this night had definitely not been a waste.

He stood silhouetted in the doorway, reminding her that she'd come with the most handsome man at the party. Suspect or not, Jordan Cardwell was a pretty good date, she thought as he drew her into his arms and out on the dance floor.

Out of the corner of her eye she saw that Shelby had Tessa in the corner. Liza meet Tessa's gaze for a moment before the woman shoved away from Shelby and dragged Wyatt Iverson out on the floor to dance with her.

"You might want to talk to Paul Henderson," Jordan said, as they were leaving the reunion party a few dances later. "Apparently, Alex asked him about the party at the cabin that night. Alex thought there were photographs taken at the party that might have something to do with Tanner's death."

"Photographs?" Liza asked. She'd settled into the SUV's passenger seat, still feeling the warmth of being in Jordan's arms on the dance floor. She'd had fun even though she hated to admit it since she was supposed to be finding a murderer.

"Paul wasn't at Tanner's kegger, but he seems to think Ashley might have gone and lied about it."

"And how does all of this lead to Alex's death?" she asked, wanting to hear Jordan's take on it.

"Tanner was staying in a cabin up on the mountain to keep an eye on Iverson Construction equipment," he said as he drove. "He throws a party, the equipment gets vandalized, he gets in trouble. Malcolm Iverson, who is on the edge of bankruptcy, believes his competitor Harris Lancaster is behind the vandalism in an attempt to take over his business. Malcolm goes gunning for him, shoots Harris accidentally and goes to prison for a couple of years. When he gets out, he drowns in a boating accident." He looked over at her. "These things have to be connected and if there really are photographs from Tanner's party, then maybe they tie it all together—and explain why Tanner is dead."

"Tanner sounds like such a sensible kid," Liza said. "Why would he throw a party at the cabin with the construction equipment nearby?"

"He swore he didn't. People just started showing up. So he went with it. But after the equipment was vandalized, he felt horrible about it." He shrugged as he drove down the mountain. "I know he blamed himself."

"Was Tanner drinking a lot that night?"

Jordan sighed. "I don't know. I got drunk and left with some girl."

"So if these photographs exist, then they might not just show who was there and with whom, the photographer might have captured the vandalism on film."

"That's what I was thinking, and if Ashley's father, Harris Lancaster, was behind it, he would have good reason not to want the photographs to surface and so would Ashley."

Liza thought of the suicide scene photos in Tanner's

file, the campfire ringed with rocks, the charred beer cans, all the tracks at the scene. "If Harris was questioned about the vandalism, there should be something down at the office in the file."

"Both Malcolm Iverson and Harris Lancaster are the kind of men who would have taken the law into their own hands," Jordan said. "And so are their sons. I doubt either of them reported anything."

"I think I should talk to Harris Lancaster," Liza said.

"Let me go along. Just to make sure you're safe. Truth is, Lancaster is the kind of man who won't take a female deputy seriously. No offense."

"Oh, none taken," she said sarcastically. "But you've done enough, thanks. So what do you have planned tomorrow?"

He'd grinned over at her. "Worried about me?"

"Tell me I don't have any reason to be."

"Look, I'm touched but—"

"It isn't personal, so save it," she said quickly. "I have one murder on my hands, maybe two. I don't need you adding another one for me to solve."

"Don't worry, Deputy. I have no intention of getting myself killed. I'll watch my back. You do the same."

She nodded. "I'm driving up to West Yellowstone to see Brick Savage. He was the investigating marshal on Tanner's death."

"I need to go see my sister. But maybe I'll see you later tomorrow? How about dinner?"

She shook her head. "I don't think that's a good idea."

"I get it. You're afraid that over dinner I might charm you into thinking I'm harmless, if you weren't careful."

"You aren't that charming and you're far from harmless."

He grinned at that. "I'm going to take that as a compliment."

"I was sure you would."

As he drove toward her condo, he said, "Seriously, watch your back tomorrow."

WHEN THEY REACHED LIZA'S CONDO, Jordan insisted on walking her to her door.

"This really isn't necessary," she said, shaking her head at him as she dug for her key. He saw the glint of her weapon in her purse along with her badge. For a while on the dance floor, he'd forgotten she was a deputy marshal. She was merely a beautiful woman in his arms.

"A gentleman always walks his date to the door."

"This isn't a date."

"Because I'm a suspect?"

She looked up from searching in her purse for her key. He'd noticed that she'd suddenly become ill at ease when he'd driven up in front of her condo. Now she froze as he moved closer until they were a breath apart.

"Do you really think I'm dangerous?" he asked.

Her laugh sounded nervous. "Absolutely."

"Well, date or not, I had fun with you," he whispered and kissed her gently. She still hadn't moved when he drew back to look into her beautiful green eyes.

He knew he should leave it at one quick kiss, turn and walk away, but there was something so alluring about her that he gripped her waist and pulled her to him. This time he kissed her like he'd wanted to since the day he'd seen her sitting astride her horse, watching him from the darkness of the trees. There'd been something mysterious and sensual about her even when he'd realized who she was.

Now she melted into him, her hands going to his shoulders, her lips parting, a soft moan escaping from deep within her.

He felt his own desire spark and catch flame. It had been so long since he'd felt like this, if he ever had before. Liza was slight in stature, but had curves in all the right places. There was something solid and real about her. He couldn't help thinking how different she was from his ex, Jill. Jill ate like a bird. If she'd consumed even a portion of the food Liza'd had tonight at the dinner, she'd be anxious to get inside the condo and throw it all up. He'd gotten so sick of her constant dieting and complaining about the way she looked.

Liza was so different from any woman he'd ever known. She knew who she was and what she wanted. She looked perfect as she was, felt perfect. He wanted to sweep her into his arms, take her inside and make love to her until daylight.

AT THE SOUND OF A VEHICLE coming up the street, Liza pushed back from the kiss as if coming up for air. She was breathing hard, her heart pounding, desire making her blood run hot.

As a white SUV slowly drove past, she saw the woman behind the wheel and swore.

"Shelby," she said, mentally kicking herself for not only letting this happen but also wanting it to.

Jordan turned to watch the vehicle disappear down the street. "Sorry."

It was bad enough that a lot of people didn't think a woman could do this job. She'd only made it worse by letting someone like Shelby see her kissing Jordan Cardwell.

"I should never have gone to the reunion dinner with you," she said.

"You were working."

"That kiss wasn't work."

"No," he said and grinned at her.

"Go home," she said.

He raised both hands and took a step back. "You want to pick me up at the cabins or should I meet you tomorrow to—"

"I already told you. I can handle this without your help."

He stopped. "Liza, I'm not giving up until Alex's killer is caught."

"It's too dangerous."

He studied her for a moment. "Too dangerous for who?" he asked, stepping to her again. He cupped the side of her face with one of his large hands. She was surprised to feel the calluses. Taking his hand, she held it to the light.

"I thought you worked on Wall Street?" she asked, hating the suspicion she heard in her voice. Worse, that Jordan had heard it.

"I used to. I quit. I've been working construction for a few years now."

"Do you even live in New York City?"

He shook his head. "Why are you getting so upset?"

"Because I've run background checks on everyone involved in this case—except *you*."

"Because you know I didn't kill Alex."

"Do I?" She glared at him, although it was herself she was angry with.

He held up his hands again. "I'm sorry if one little kiss—"

"It wasn't one little kiss," she snapped and closed her eyes as she realized what she'd said. The kiss had shaken her. Worse, it had sparked a desire in her for this man, of all men.

"Run your background check. Do whatever it is you have to do," he said as he took a step away. "I have nothing to hide. But know this. That wasn't just some little kiss for me, either. If I had my way, I'd have you inside that condo and I'd be taking off your clothes right now. Good night, Deputy Marshal. I had a nice time. You make a nice date."

With that, he turned and walked to his vehicle while she stood trembling on the condo stoop thinking about what he'd said. Imagining the two of them tearing at each other's clothing. She knew that if he had taken her inside, they would have never made it to the bedroom.

As he drove away, she stood breathing in the cold night air, trying to still the aching need inside her. She'd always prided herself on her strength and determination. Nothing had kept her from realizing her goal to get where she was now. That had meant not letting a man either slow her down or stop her dead in her pursuit.

She wasn't going to let Jordan Cardwell ruin not just her reputation, but her credibility as a deputy marshal. The realization that she wanted him as much as he wanted her shocked her. No man had ever interested her enough for the problem to come up before. She reminded herself that Jordan was a suspect.

After a moment she dug into her purse until she found her key. With shaking fingers, she unlocked the door and stepped inside.

Even before she turned on the light, she knew something was terribly wrong. Someone had ransacked her condo.

She stood staring at the mess, trying to make sense of it. Why would someone do this? Her heart began to pound. This felt as if it was a warning.

Or had someone been looking for something and not finding it, just decided to tear the place up? Were they looking for the photographs Alex had been asking about?

Either way, she felt as if she'd gotten the message. Unfortunately, she'd never been good at heeding these kinds of warnings.

If anything, she was more determined than ever to solve this case and get Jordan Cardwell off her suspect list.

Chapter Ten

Saturday morning after cleaning up her condo, Liza drove up the canyon. It was one of those amazing Montana fall days. The sky was robin's-egg blue and not a cloud was in sight. The deciduous trees along the river glowed in bright blinding golds and deep reds next to the dark green of the pines.

At the heart of it all was the Gallatin River, running clear and beautiful, as it wound through the canyon and rocks. Harris Lancaster lived in a large modern home that looked as if it had been picked up in some big city and accidentally dropped here by the river.

His wife answered the door and pointed Liza toward a building a ways from the house. She followed a graveled path to the door and knocked.

Harris was a big burly brisk man with a loud deep voice and piercing gray eyes. Liza tried to imagine him in the very feminine furnishings of the house she'd glimpsed before his wife had closed the door.

His office looked like him, large and messy. The space was taken up by everything from dirty outdoor clothing and piles of papers and building plans to equipment parts and an old couch that Liza suspected he probably slept on more often than not. Given the pristine look of the house and Malcolm's wife, Liza doubted he was allowed to set foot inside it.

He cleared off an old wooden chair, motioned her into it and took a seat behind his cluttered desk. "So what's this about?" The office smelled of cigar smoke.

"I want to talk to you about Tanner Cole," Liza said.

"Who?"

"He worked for Malcolm Iverson twenty years ago when he was in high school."

He laughed. "*Seriously?* I can't remember who works for me right now, why would I remember who worked for Malcolm?"

"Tanner committed suicide twenty years ago after Malcolm Iverson's construction equipment was vandalized. It was just days before Malcolm shot you and went to prison."

He shook his head. "I try not to think about any of that."

"Tanner was in the same class as your daughter Ashley. He lived in a cabin near the construction site. Malcolm held Tanner responsible, but ultimately, he believed you were behind the vandalism that forced him into bankruptcy."

He scoffed at that. "Malcolm didn't know anything about running a business. He spent too much time in the bar. But I had nothing to do with vandalizing his equipment. He was just looking for someone to blame. Anyway, I heard the vandalism was kid stuff. You know, sugar in the gas tanks, broken and missing motor parts. Pure mischief. That's what happens when you get a bunch of drunk kids together."

"Or it was made to look like kids did it," she noted, but Harris Lancaster didn't seem to be listening.

"I do remember something about that Tanner boy now that you mention it. Ashley was real upset. We all were," he added. "Tanner's family has a ranch on the way to West Yellowstone. Too bad, but I don't see what any of that has to do with me."

"You benefited by Malcolm going broke."

He shrugged. "Maybe, at the time. But there was plenty of work to go around. His son and I are competitors, but we aren't shooting each other and we're both doing quite well."

He had a point. Maybe his problems with Malcolm and vice versa had nothing to do with Tanner's death. Maybe it had been guilt. Or maybe there were some photographs somewhere that told a different story.

JORDAN PULLED UP OUT IN FRONT of the house where he'd been raised. He sat for a moment just looking at the large two-story house. The other day when he'd come into town, he'd driven in from the other side of the ranch to make sure no one was at home before he'd come down to borrow a hat.

At least that had been his excuse. He'd wanted to wander around the house without anyone watching him. He knew his sister would think he was casing the joint, looking for valuables he could pawn or sell on eBay.

He and Dana had always butted heads, although he wished that wasn't the case. He'd always respected her. She worked harder than anyone he knew and made the rest of them feel like slackers.

Even after the good luck he'd had after Jill had left, he still felt like he could never measure up to Dana. Now as he opened his car door and climbed out, he half expected Dana to meet him on the porch. Possibly with a shotgun in her hands. Then he remembered that Hud had said she was pregnant with twins and having a hard time.

At the door, he knocked. It felt strange to knock at a door he'd run in and out of for years.

To his surprise, Stacy opened the door. He'd thought she was just passing through. But then again that would explain the beater car with the California plates he now saw parked off to the side. He hadn't even noticed it he'd been so busy looking at the house.

"Stacy," he said, unable to hide his surprise.

"Jordan?" She put a lot into that one word.

"It's all right. I didn't come by to cause trouble. I just wanted to see my sister. Sisters," he corrected. "And my niece and nephew."

"Nieces," she said and stepped back to let him come in.

"That's right. Hud said you have a baby?"

"Don't sound so surprised." Stacy studied him for a moment. "I'll see if Dana is up to having company."

"I'm not company. I'm *family*."

She lifted an eyebrow as if to say, "Since when?"

As if *she* should talk, he thought as she headed for the downstairs sunroom that had been their parent's bedroom, then their mother's and now apparently Dana's.

"Where are the kids?" he called after Stacy.

She shot him a warning look. "Down for their naps."

"Sorry," he whispered. He stood in the doorway, afraid to step in and feeling badly that it had come to this.

Stacy returned a moment later. She didn't look happy. "Dana isn't supposed to be upset."

"Thanks for the warning," he said and stepped across the living room to the doorway Stacy had just come from.

He stopped the moment he saw Dana. She looked beautiful, propped up against an array of pillows. Their gazes locked and he stepped the rest of the way into the room, closing the door behind him.

"Hey, sis," he said.

"Jordan." She began to cry.

With a lump in his throat at her reaction, he closed the distance and bent down to hug her awkwardly. "Are you all right?" he asked pulling back to look at her. "You look…beautiful."

"I thought you were going to say…big," she said laughing and crying as she wiped at her eyes. "It's the hormones," she said pointing at her tears. "I cry over everything."

"That explains it. For a minute there I thought you might have missed me," he said as he pulled up the chair next to the bed.

She stopped drying her tears to meet his gaze. "You seem…different."

He smiled. "Oh, I'm still that stubborn, temperamental brother you remember. But maybe some of the hard edges have gotten knocked off."

Dana nodded. "Maybe that's it. Hud told me why you were in town."

"I didn't think you wanted to see me or I would have come by sooner."

"You're my older brother."

"Exactly," he only half joked.

The bedroom door opened. Stacy stuck her head in.

"I think I'll run that errand I told you about yesterday. The kids are still down. Should I move Ella?"

"No, I'll have Jordan bring her in before he leaves."

Stacy looked to her brother as if she wasn't sure that was a good idea.

"I haven't dropped a baby all day," he said.

"And Hud should be back any minute," Dana said to reassure her sister.

Stacy mugged a face at him and closed the door. He listened to her leave. But it wasn't until they both couldn't hear her old beater car engine any longer before they spoke.

"I did a lot of soul searching after everything that happened," he said. "I'm sorry."

"Me too."

"I went up to the cemetery and saw Mom the first day I got here. I borrowed a hat. Nothing else," he added quickly.

"Jordan, this ranch is your home too."

"I know, sis," he said putting a hand on her arm. "Mom always thought I'd come back and want to help you ranch."

Dana chuckled at that. "She said Stacy and Clay were gone, but you...well, she said there was ranching in your blood."

"Yeah. So tell me what's going on with you."

She placed her hands over her huge stomach. "I'm on bed rest with these two for the last weeks. I'm going insane."

He laughed. "I can imagine. And Stacy is...?"

"She's been great. Mary and Hank adore her."

"Mary and Hank. I can't wait to meet them."

"You should come back for dinner tonight," Dana said.

He shook his head. "Not sure that's a good idea given the way your husband feels about me, not to mention everything else going on right now."

"I wish you would. At least once before you leave," Dana said, tearing up again.

"You and your hormones." He got up and hugged her again. Straightening to leave, he asked, "So where's this baby I'm supposed to bring you before I leave?"

At the sound of the front door opening, Dana said, "Sounds like Hud's home. You'll have to come back to meet Ella."

"I'll try. You take care of yourself and your babies." As he opened the door, he came face to face with his brother-in-law again. "I was just leaving and no, I didn't upset her."

Hud looked past him to Dana. "What is she crying about then?"

"It's just the hormones," Dana said.

Jordan shrugged. "Just the hormones."

As he left, he found himself looking toward the barn, remembering his childhood here. Amazing how the place looked so different from the way he remembered it the last time he was here. Had he really tried to force his sister into selling it, lock, stock and barrel?

He felt a wave of shame as he walked to his rental SUV and climbed inside.

"WHERE'S STACY?" HUD ASKED as he stuck his head in the bedroom door later.

Dana saw that he had Ella on one shoulder. She realized she'd fallen asleep after Jordan had left and had awakened a few moments ago when she'd heard the baby cry.

"She said she wanted to go see Angus," Dana said groggily as she pulled herself up a little in the bed. "She said she wouldn't be gone long." Glancing at the clock beside her bed, she was shocked to see what time it was. "She hasn't come back?"

Hud shook his head. "I just changed Ella. I was going to heat some formula for her." He sounded worried.

Past him, Dana could see that it was dark outside. She felt a flutter of apprehension. "Stacy should have been back by now. Here, I'll take the baby. Call my father. Maybe they got to visiting and she just lost track of time."

"The kids and I are making dinner." Hud handed her Ella. "They ordered beanie wienies."

"Sounds great." She could smell the bacon and onions sizzling in the skillet. But her gaze was on the baby in her arms. Ella smiled up at her and she felt her heart do a somersault. Stacy was just running late. She probably didn't remember how quickly it got dark this time of year in the canyon.

A few minutes later, Hud came into the bedroom. "I called your father. He hasn't seen Stacy."

She felt her heart drop, but hid her fear as the kids came running in excitedly chanting "beanie wienies."

Hud set up Mary and Hank's small table in the bedroom so they could all eat dinner with her. The beanie wienies were wonderful. They finished the meal off with some of the brownies Aunt Stacy had made.

"Is Auntie Stacy going to live with us?" Mary asked.

"No, she's just visiting," Dana told her daughter. There was still no sign of Stacy. No call. Dana found herself listening, praying for the sound of her old car coming up the road. But there was only silence. "I'm not sure how long your aunt can stay."

Hank looked over at Ella who was drooling and laughing as she tried to roll over on the other side of the bed. "She can't leave without her baby," he said. "Can she?"

She shot Hud a look. Could Stacy leave without her baby?

"I'm going to call Hilde and see if she can come over while I go look for Stacy," Hud said. "I called Liza but she's in West Yellowstone. Apparently, she went up there to talk to my father about the case she's working."

Dana nodded, seeing her own worry reflected in his face.

"I'll call you if I hear anything." Big Sky was relatively small. Stacy couldn't have gone far. Unless she'd changed her mind about seeing their father and gone into Bozeman for some reason. But she'd said she would be back before Ella woke up from her nap. What if something had happened to her sister?

Trying to rein in her fear, Dana told the kids to get a game for them all to play.

"Ella can't play, Mommy," Mary cried. "She'll eat the game pieces."

"No, Ella will just watch," she told her daughter as she fought the dread that Stacy hadn't changed at all.

In that case Dana hated to think what that might mean. That Stacy wouldn't be back? Or worse, she'd left her baby. If it was her baby.

Chapter Eleven

Jordan felt at loose ends after leaving his sister's. On impulse he drove as far as he could up the road to the construction site where he'd found Tanner that horrible morning twenty years before.

The road was now paved and led up to a massive home. He could tell from the looks of it that the owner wasn't around and probably didn't come up but for a few weeks in the winter and summer.

The house had been built on a cleared area high on the mountain where the construction equipment had been parked twenty years ago. The small log cabin where Tanner had lived was gone. So was the campfire ring. Nothing looked as it had except for the tree where he'd found Tanner hanging that spring day.

There was also no sign that this was the spot where his best friend had taken his life. No log stumps. No rope mark on the large old pine limb. Nothing left of the tragedy even on the breeze that moaned in the high boughs. Jordan doubted the place's owners knew about the death that had occurred within yards of their vacation home.

He felt a sadness overwhelm him. "Why, Tanner? Why the hell did you do it?" he demanded as he looked up at the large limb where he'd found him. "Or did you?" He feared they would never know as he looked again at the dried-pine-needle-covered ground. Did he really think he was going to find answers up here?

Too antsy to go back to his cabin, he drove up the canyon. When he saw his father's truck parked outside The Corral, he swung in. He found his father and uncle sitting on their usual stools at the bar.

"Son? I thought you would have left by now," Angus Cardwell said. "Bob, get my son a beer."

Jordan noticed there were a few men at the end of the bar and several families at the tables in the dining area eating.

Angus slapped his son on the back as Jordan slid onto a stool next to him. The bar smelled of burgers and beer. Not a bad combination, he thought, figuring he understood why his old man had such an infatuation with bars.

"What have you been up to?" Uncle Harlan asked him.

"My twenty-year class reunion," he said, figuring that would suffice.

"You actually went to it?" his father said with a laugh.

"I went with the deputy marshal."

Both older men hooted. "That's my son," Angus said proudly.

Jordan had known that would be his father's reaction. It was why he'd said it. He was just glad Liza hadn't been around to hear it.

The draft beer was cold and went down easy. Heck, he might have a burger while he was at it. He settled in, listening to the watering hole banter, a television over the bar droning in the background.

"Your deputy figured out who killed that man at the falls?" his uncle asked him.

"Not yet, but she will," he said with confidence.

His father smiled over at him and gave him a wink. "That what's really keeping you in the canyon, ain't it?"

Jordan smiled and ordered burgers for the three of them.

Later when he drove back to Big Sky and stopped by the Marshal's Office, he was disappointed to learn that Liza hadn't returned from West Yellowstone. He thought about what his father had said about his reasons for staying around. If he was being honest with himself, Liza definitely played into it.

LIZA FOUND BRICK Savage sitting on the deck of his Hebgen Lake home. She'd heard stories about him and, after he'd ignored her knocks at his front door, braced herself as she approached his deck.

"Mr. Savage?"

He looked up, his gaze like a piercing arrow as he took in her uniform first, then studied her face before saying, "Yes?"

"I'm Deputy Marshal Liza Turner out of the Big Sky office. I'd like a moment of your time."

"You have any identification?" His voice was gravelly but plenty strong.

She pulled her ID and climbed a couple of steps so he could see it.

He nodded, amusement in his gaze. "Deputy Marshal. Times really have changed. I heard my son left you in charge of the murder case."

"That's correct."

"Well, come on up here then," Brick said and pushed himself up out of his chair. He was a big man, but she could see that he used to be a lot bigger in his younger days. There was a no-nonsense aura about him along with his reputation that made her a little nervous being in his company.

He shoved a chair toward her as she reached the deck and waited for her to sit before he pulled up a weather-grayed log stump and settled himself on it.

"I hate to take your chair," she said, wondering about a man who had only one chair on his deck. Apparently he didn't expect or get much company. Did that mean he didn't see much of Hud and family?

"So?" Brick said as if his time was valuable and she was wasting it.

"I want to ask you about Tanner Cole's death. He was a senior—"

"I know who he was. Found hanging from a tree up on the side of the mountain overlooking Big Sky twenty-odd years ago," Brick said. "What do you want to know?"

"Was it a suicide?"

He leveled his gaze at her. "Wasn't it ruled one?"

"At the time. Is it possible Tanner had help?"

"It's always possible. Was there any sign of a struggle like scratches or bruises? Not according to the coroner's report but if you did your homework, you'd already know that. As for footprints, there were a lot of them. He'd had a beer bash, kegger, whatever your generation calls it. He'd had that within a few days so there were all kinds of tracks at the scene."

She knew all this and wondered if she'd wasted her

time driving all the way up here. Past him she could see the deep green of the lake, feel a cold breeze coming off the water. Clouds had already gathered over Lion's Head Mountain, one of the more recognizable ones seen from his deck. Add to that the sun had already gone down. As it was, it would be dark before she got back to Big Sky.

"I can tell you this, he used his own rope," Brick said.

She nodded. "What about Jordan Cardwell?"

"What about him?"

"You found him at the scene. Is there any chance—"

"He didn't kill his friend, if that's what you're asking."

"You're that sure?" she said, hearing the relief in her voice and suspecting he did too. She'd started to like Jordan, suspect or not. She knew it was a bad idea on so many levels, but there was something about him...

"What did you really come up here to ask me?" Brick demanded.

"I guess what I want is your gut reaction."

"My gut reaction isn't worth squat. Do I think he killed himself?" The former marshal shrugged. "Strangulation takes a while. Gives a man a lot of time to reconsider and change his mind, but with all his body weight on the rope, it's impossible to get your fingers under the rope and relieve the pressure."

She looked at him in surprise. "Are you telling me he—"

"Changed his mind and clawed at the rope?" He nodded.

"Why wasn't that in the coroner's report?"

"It's not uncommon. But also not something a family member ever wants to know about. I would imagine Rupert wanted to spare them any more pain."

Liza shook her head. "But couldn't it also mean that Tanner Cole never meant to hang himself? That someone else put that rope around his neck?"

"And he didn't fight until that person kicked the log out?" Brick asked. "Remember, there were no defensive wounds or marks on his body."

"Maybe he thought it was a joke."

The elderly former marshal studied her for a moment. "What would make you let someone put a noose around your neck, joking or otherwise?"

That was the question, wasn't it?

"You think he killed himself," she said.

He shrugged. "Prove me wrong."

HUD SPENT A GOOD TWO HOURS canvassing the area for his sister-in-law before he put out the APB on her vehicle. He checked with the main towing services first though, telling himself her car could have broken down. All kinds of things could have happened to detain her—and maybe even keep her from calling.

But after those two hours he knew in his gut that wasn't the case. Stacy had split.

At the office he did something he'd hoped he wouldn't have to do. He began checking again for kidnappings of children matching Ella's description and realized he needed to narrow his search. Since Stacy was driving a car with California plates...

He realized he should have run her plates first. Feeling only a little guilty for having taken down her license number when he'd first become suspicious of her, he brought up his first surprise.

The car had been registered in La Jolla, California—but not to Stacy by any of her former married names or her maiden name of Cardwell.

The car was registered to Clay Cardwell—her brother.

He picked up the phone and called the family lawyer who was handling the dispersing of ranch profits to Dana's siblings.

"Rick, I hate to bother you, but I need to get a phone number and address for Dana's brother Clay. I understand he's living in La Jolla, California."

Rick cleared his voice. "Actually I was going to contact Dana, but hesitated when I heard she's on bed rest at the ranch pregnant with the twins."

News traveled fast, Hud thought. "What's up?" he asked, afraid he wasn't going to like it.

"Clay. He hasn't been cashing his checks. It's been going on for about six months. I just assumed he might be holding them for some reason. But the last one came back saying there was no one by that name and no forwarding address."

Hud swore under his breath. Six months. The same age as Ella. Although he couldn't imagine what the two things could have in common or why Clay hadn't cashed his checks or how it was that his older sister was driving a car registered to him.

"I think we need to find him," Hud said. "I'd just as soon Dana didn't know anything about this. Believe me, she has her hands full right now. One more thing though. Stacy. Did she give you a new address to send her checks?"

"No. She's moved around so much, I wait until I hear from her and usually send them general delivery."

"Well, could you do me a favor? If you hear from her, call me."

"I thought she was here in the canyon."

"She was, but right now she's missing and she left a small…package at the house."

IT WAS DARK BY THE TIME LIZA drove past the Fir Ridge cemetery, climbed up over the Continental Divide and entered Gallatin Canyon.

This time of year there was little traffic along the two-lane road as it snaked through pines and over mountains along the edge of the river.

She kept thinking about what Brick Savage had told her. More to the point, the feeling she'd had when she'd left him. He'd challenged her to prove Tanner Cole had been murdered. No doubt because he knew it would be near impossible.

And yet if she was right and Alex's murder had something to do with Tanner's death, then the killer had shown his hand.

Pulling out her phone, she tried Hud's cell. In a lot of spots in the canyon there was no mobile phone service. To her surprise it began to ring.

"Marshal Savage," he snapped.

"Sorry, did I catch you at a bad time?" she asked through the hands-free speaker, wondering if he was in the middle of something with the kids.

"Liza. Good. I'm glad you called. Did you get my message?"

She hadn't. Fear gripped her. Surely there hadn't been another murder. Her thoughts instantly raced to Jordan and she felt her heart fall at the thought that he might—

"It's Stacy," he said. "She left the house earlier. No one has seen her since. She hasn't called. I've looked all over Big Sky. She left the baby at the house."

"What?" It took her moment to pull back from the thought of another murder. To pull back from the fear and dread that had had her thinking something had happened to Jordan. "Stacy wouldn't leave her baby, would she?"

"Knowing Stacy, I have a bad feeling the baby isn't even hers."

Liza was too shocked to speak for a moment. "You think she…stole it?"

"Something is wrong. I've suspected it from the get-go. Dana was hoping I was just being suspicious because it's my nature, but I'd been worried that something like this would happen. I didn't want Dana getting attached to that baby, but you know Dana, and Ella is adorable, if that is even her name."

"Oh, boss, I'm so sorry."

"So you spoke to my father?" Hud asked.

"He was the investigating officer at Tanner Cole's suicide."

"What did he tell you?"

"That it was Tanner's rope."

Hud let out a humorless laugh. "That sounds like Brick. Have you met him before?"

"Never had the honor. He must have been a treat as a father."

"You could say that." He sighed. "Look, Hilde's at the house. I'm going to make another circle through the area to look for Stacy before I go home."

"I'm about twenty minutes out. Do you want me to stop by?"

"If you don't mind. I know you're busy with this murder case…"

"No problem. I'll see you soon." She snapped the phone shut, shocked by what he'd told her. She was so deep in thought that she hadn't noticed the lights of another vehicle coming up behind her.

She glanced in the mirror. One of the headlights was out on the approaching car. That struck her about the same time as she realized the driver was coming up too fast.

She'd been going the speed limit. By now the driver of the vehicle behind her would have been able to see the light bar on the top of her SUV. Only a fool would come racing up on a Marshal's Department patrol car—let alone pass it.

And yet as she watched, the driver of what appeared to be an old pickup swerved around her and roared up beside her.

Liza hit her lights and siren, thinking the driver must be drunk. She glanced over, saw only a dark figure behind the wheel wearing a black ski mask. Her heart jumped, but she didn't have time to react before the driver swerved into her. She heard the crunch of metal, felt the patrol SUV veer toward the ditch and the pines and beyond that, the river.

She slammed on the brakes, but was traveling too fast to avoid the truck crashing into her again. The force made the vehicle rock wildly as she fought to keep control. The tires screamed on the pavement as the SUV began to fishtail.

Liza felt the right side of the vehicle dip into the soft shoulder of the highway, pulling the SUV off the road. She couldn't hold it and felt her tires leave the pavement. A stand of trees blurred past and then there was nothing but darkness as she plunged over the edge of the road toward the dark green of the river.

Chapter Twelve

Hud was headed home when he heard the 911 call for an ambulance come over his radio. His heart began to race as he heard that the vehicle in the river was a Montana marshal's patrol SUV.

He threw on his siren and lights and took off up the canyon toward West Yellowstone. As he raced toward the accident, he called home, glad when Hilde answered the phone.

"Tell Dana I'm running a little late," he said to Hilde. "Don't act like anything is wrong." He heard Dana already asking what was going on. Hilde related the running a little late part.

"We're just fine," Hilde said.

"It sounds like there's been an accident up the canyon," he told her. "It's Liza. I don't know anything except that her car is in the river. I don't know how long I'm going to be."

"Don't worry about us."

"Is it my sister?" Dana demanded in the background.

"I heard that. Tell her I haven't found Stacy. I'll call when I have news. I just don't want Dana upset."

"Got it. I'll tell her."

He disconnected and increased his speed. Liza was

like family. How the hell did she end up in the river? She was a great driver.

As he came around a bend in the windy road, he saw her patrol SUV among the boulders in the Gallatin River. Some bypassers had stopped. Several of the men had flashlights and one of them had waded out to the patrol vehicle.

Hud parked, leaving his lights on to warn any oncoming traffic, then grabbing his own flashlight, jumped out and ran toward the river. As he dropped over the edge of the road to it, he recognized the man who was standing on the boulder beside Liza's wrecked vehicle.

"Jordan?" he called.

"Liza's conscious," he called back. "An ambulance is on the way. I'm staying with her until it gets here."

Hud would have liked to have gone to her as well, but he heard the sound of the ambulance siren and climbed back up the road to help with traffic control.

All the time, though, he found himself wondering how Jordan just happened to be on the scene.

"WHAT'S HAPPENED?" DANA demanded the moment Hilde hung up. "Don't," she said before Hilde could open her mouth. "You're a terrible liar and we both know it. Tell me."

"He hasn't found your sister."

She nodded. "But something else has happened."

"There's been an accident up the canyon. He needed to run up there."

Dana waited. "There's more."

"You're the one who should have gone into law enforcement, the interrogation part," Hilde said as she came and sat down on the edge of the bed. On the other side of Dana, baby Ella slept, looking like an angel. Hilde glanced at the baby, then took Dana's hand as if she knew it was only a matter of time before her friend got the truth out of her. "Hud didn't know anything about the accident except that Liza is somehow involved."

"Oh, no." Her heart dropped.

"Now don't get upset and have these babies because Hud will never forgive me," Hilde said quickly.

Dana shook her head. "I'm okay. But I want to know the minute you hear something. Are you sure you can stay?"

"Of course."

"You didn't have a date?"

Hilde laughed. "If only there were more Hudson Savages around. All of the men I meet, well…they're so not the kind of men I want to spend time with, even for the time it takes to have dinner."

"I *am* lucky." Dana looked over at Ella. "What if Hud is right and Ella isn't Stacy's baby?"

"Where would she have gotten Ella? You can't just get a baby off eBay."

"She could have *kidnapped* Ella. You know Stacy."

"I'm sure Hud checked for any kidnapped babies six months old with dimples, blond hair and green eyes," Hilde argued.

"Yes, green eyes. You might have noticed that all the Justices have dark brown eyes and dark hair, including Stacy."

"Maybe the father has green eyes and Stacy carries a green-eyed gene. You don't know that Ella isn't Stacy's."

"No," Dana admitted, but like Hud, she'd had a bad

feeling since the moment Stacy had arrived. "I think Stacy only came here because she's in trouble and it has something to do with that poor little baby."

"You think that's why she left Ella with you?"

Dana fingered the quilt edge where someone had stitched the name Katie. "I wish I knew."

JORDAN WOKE WITH A CRICK in his neck. He stared down at the green hospital scrubs he was wearing for a moment, confused where he was. It came back to him with a start. Last night his clothes had been soaking wet from his swim in the river. He'd been shivering uncontrollably, but had refused to leave the hospital until he knew Liza was going to be all right.

That's how he'd ended up in scrubs, he recalled now as he sat up in the chair beside Liza's bed and smiled at the woman propped up staring at him now.

"What are you still doing here?" she asked, smiling.

"I *was* sleeping." He stood up, stretched, then looked to see what she was having for breakfast. "You haven't eaten much," he said as he took a piece of toast from the nearly untouched tray.

"I'm not very hungry."

He was famished and realized he hadn't eaten since yesterday at noon. "How are your ribs?" he asked as he devoured the piece of toast.

"They're just bruised and only hurt when I breathe."

"Yep, but you're breathing. Be thankful for that."

Liza nodded and he saw that her left wrist was also wrapped. Apparently, it was just badly sprained, not broken. His big worry, though, had been that she'd suffered internal injuries.

Apparently not, though, since all she had was a bandage on her right temple, a bruised cheek and a scrape on her left cheek. She'd been lucky.

"So what did the doctor say?" he asked.

"That I'm going to live."

"Good."

She looked almost shy. "Thank you for last night."

He shrugged. "It's wasn't anything. I just swam a raging river in October in Montana and clung onto a slippery boulder to be with you." He grinned. "I'm just glad you're all right." He'd been forced to leave the room last night while Hud had talked to her, but he'd overheard enough to more than concern him.

"You said last night that someone forced you off the road?" he asked now. "Do you remember anything about the vehicle?"

She narrowed her gaze at him and sighed. "Even if I knew who did it, I wouldn't tell you. I don't want to see you get killed."

He grinned. "Nice that you care—"

"I told you, I don't have time to find your killer, too."

"Why would anyone want to kill me? On second thought, scratch that. Other than my brother-in-law, why would anyone want me dead?"

"Hud doesn't want you dead."

"He just doesn't want me near my sister."

"Can you blame him?"

"No," he said with a sigh. "That's what makes it worse. I would be the same way if someone had treated my wife the way I've treated my sister." He looked away.

"Do you mean that?"

He grinned. "Do you question everything I tell you?"

"Yes."

He laughed and shook his head. "I've been more

honest with you than I have with anyone in a very long time. Hud doesn't want me near you, either." He met her gaze and saw something warm flash in her eyes.

"I talked to the investigating officer in Tanner's death yesterday before the accident," she said, clearly changing the subject. "He cleared you as a suspect, at least in Tanner's death."

"Did Brick Savage tell you what I did the day I found Tanner?"

"I would assume you were upset since it was your best friend."

"I broke down and bawled like a baby until Hud's old man kicked me in the behind and told me to act like a man. He said I was making myself look guilty as hell." He chuckled. "I took a swing at him and he decked me. Knocked me on my butt, but I got control of myself after that and he didn't arrest me for assaulting an officer of the law so I guess I respect him for that."

Liza shook her head. "Men. You are such a strange breed. I think it would have been stranger if you hadn't reacted the way you had."

He shrugged. "Tanner left a hole in my life. I've never had a closer friend since. Sometimes I swear I can hear his voice, especially when I do something stupid."

She smiled. "So he's still with you a lot."

"Yeah. You do know that when I say I hear him, I don't really *hear* him, right?"

"I get it."

"I didn't want you to think I hear voices. It's bad enough you still see me as a suspect."

She nodded slowly. "I mean what I said about wanting you to be safe. You need to keep a low profile."

"How can I do that when I have a reunion picnic to go to this afternoon?"

"You aren't seriously planning to go?"

"What? You don't think I can get another date?" he joked.

"What do I have to do to make you realize how dangerous this is?"

His expression sobered. "All I have to do is look at your face and think about where I found you last night."

"You could be next," she said quietly. "What time is the picnic?"

"The doctor isn't going to let you—"

"What time?" she demanded.

"One."

"I'll be there."

He grinned. "Good, I won't have to find another date." He wanted to argue that she needed to stay in bed. He couldn't stand the thought that she was now a target. Last night when he'd seen her car in the river— Just the thought made it hard for him to breathe even now.

He barely remembered throwing on the rental car's brakes, diving out and half falling down the bank to the river. All he could think about was getting to her. The moment he'd hit the icy water of the Gallatin, he'd almost been swept away. He'd had to swim to get to her, then climb onto a large slick boulder to reach the driver's-side door.

At first he'd thought she was dead. There was blood from the cut on her temple.

Impulsively, he reached for her hand now. It felt warm and soft and wonderfully alive. He squeezed her hand gently, then let it go.

"Unless you need a ride, I guess I'll see you at one on the mountain then," he said and turned to leave.

"Liza isn't going anywhere, especially with you," Hud snapped as he stepped into the hospital room. "I'll speak to *you* in the hall," he said to Jordan.

Liza shot him a questioning look. Jordan shrugged. He had no idea why his brother-in-law was angry with him but he was about to find out.

"Later," he said to Liza and stepped out in the hall to join Hud.

The marshal had blood in his eye by the time Jordan stepped out into the hall. "What were you doing at the accident last night? Were you following Liza?"

He held up his hands. "One question at a time. I had tried to call her. I knew she'd gone up to West Yellowstone to talk to your father. I got tired of waiting for her to return and drove up the canyon. I was worried about her."

"Worried about her?" Hud sighed. "And you just happened to find her?"

"The other driver who stopped can verify it."

"Did you pass another vehicle coming from the direction of the accident?"

"Several. A white van. A semi. An old red pickup."

"The red pickup. Did you happen to notice the driver?"

He shook his head. "I just glanced at the vehicles. I wasn't paying a lot of attention since I was looking for Liza's patrol SUV. You think the truck ran her off the road."

Hud didn't look happy to hear that Jordan knew about that. He ignored the statement and asked, "Where is Liza going to meet you later?"

"At the reunion picnic up on the mountain."

"Well, she's not going anywhere." Hud started to turn away, but swung back around and put a finger in Jordan's face. "I want you to stay away from her. I'm not sure what your game is—"

"There's *no* game. No angle. Liza is investigating Alex Winslow's murder. I've been helping her because I know the players and I think it is somehow tied in with Tanner's death."

"That better be all there is to it," Hud said and started to turn away again.

"What if that isn't all it is?" Jordan demanded, then could have kicked himself.

Hud turned slowly back to him. "Like I said, stay away from Liza." With that, he turned and pushed into his deputy's room.

"Tell me you weren't out in the hall threatening the man who saved me last night," Jordan heard Liza say, but didn't catch Hud's reply, which was just as well.

He collected his clothes at the nurse's station, changed and headed for the canyon and Big Sky. Now more than ever he wanted to get to the bottom of this. Someone had tried to kill Liza. He didn't doubt they would try again.

But what were they so afraid she was going to find out? He suddenly recalled something he'd overheard Hud say to his deputy marshal last night at the hospital. Something about her condo being ransacked. Someone thought she had something. The alleged photographs?

LIZA COCKED HER HEAD at her boss as he came around the end of her bed. "Well?" she asked.

He gave her a sheepish look. "You don't know Jordan like I do. He's…he's…"

"He's changed."

Hud shook his head. "I really doubt that he's changed any more than his sister Stacy."

"Talk about painting them all with the same brush," she said.

"Look, I don't want you getting involved with him."

Liza grinned. "I'm sorry, I must have misheard you. You weren't telling me who I can get involved with, were you, boss?"

"Damn it, Liza. You know how I feel about you."

She nodded. "I'm the most stubborn deputy you've ever had. I often take things in my own hands without any thought to my safety. I'm impulsive, emotional and driven and I'm too smart for my own good. Does that about cover it?"

"You're the best law officer I've ever worked with," Hud said seriously. "And a friend. And like a real sister to my wife. I just don't want to see you get hurt."

She smiled. "I can also take care of myself. And," she said before he could interrupt, "I can get involved with anyone I want."

He looked at his boots before looking at her again. "You're right."

"That's what I thought. Did you bring the information I asked for?" she asked, pointing to the manila envelope in his hand and no longer wanting to discuss Jordan.

Truthfully she didn't know how she felt about him—waking up to see him sleeping beside her hospital bed or being in his arms the other night on the dance floor.

"I brought it," Hud said with a sigh. "But I don't

think you should be worrying about any of this right now. How are you feeling?"

"Fine," Liza said, reaching for the manila envelope and quickly opening it.

"There are Alex's phone calls over the past month as well as where he went after arriving at Big Sky."

Liza was busy leafing through it, more determined than ever to find out who'd killed him—and who'd tried to do the same to her the night before.

"Alex was in the middle of a contentious divorce?" she asked, looking up in surprise from the information he'd brought her. "He had a *wife?*" When she'd notified next of kin, she'd called his brother as per the card in his wallet.

"Her name is Crystal."

"A classmate?"

Hud nodded. "But not from Big Sky. She lived down in Bozeman."

"What was holding up the divorce?" Liza asked.

He shook his head and had to take a step back from the bed as Liza swung her legs over the side and stood up. *"What are you doing?"*

"I'm getting up. I told you, I'm fine. Just a little knock on the head and a few cuts and bruises and a sprained wrist, but it's my left wrist, so I'm fine. All I need is a vehicle."

He shook his head. "I can't allow—"

"You can't stop me. Someone tried to *kill* me. This has become personal. Not only that, you need to stay close to home," she said as she rummaged in the closet for her clothes. "No sign of Stacy yet?" He shook his head. "What about the baby?"

"The lab's running a DNA test. We should be able

to tell if the baby is Stacy's by comparing Ella's DNA to Dana's. Liza, you're really not up to—"

"Could you see about my clothes?" she asked, realizing they weren't anywhere in the room. Her clothes had been wet and the nurses had probably taken them to dry them. "Stubborn, remember? One of the reasons I'm such a good law officer, your words not mine." She smiled widely although it hurt her face.

He studied her for a moment. "Clothes, right. Then get you a vehicle," he said, clearly giving up on trying to keep another woman in bed.

DANA WATCHED HILDE TRYING to change Ella's diaper until she couldn't take it anymore. "Give me that baby."

Hilde laughed. "You make it look so easy," she said, handing Ella to her.

Ella giggled and squirmed as Dana made short work of getting her into a diaper and a sleeper. Hud had come in so late, Hilde had stayed overnight and gotten someone to work for her this morning. He'd promised to be back soon.

"I'm just so glad Liza is all right," she said as she handed Ella back to Hilde. Through the open bedroom door she could see Mary and Hank playing with a plastic toy ranch set. She could hear them discussing whether or not they should buy more cows.

"Me, too," Hilde said. "Fortunately, Liza is strong."

"Hud's worried now that she and Jordan might be getting involved."

Hilde arched an eyebrow. "Really?"

"I have to admit when Jordan stopped by, he did seem different. But then again I said Stacy had changed, so what do I know? I can't believe we haven't heard anything from her. What if she never comes back?" Dana hadn't let herself think about that at first, but as the hours passed… "Did she leave anything else besides Ella and the baby's things?"

"I can check. She was staying in the room I slept in last night, right?"

"I would imagine Hud already checked it, but would you look? That should tell us if she was planning to leave the baby all along or if something happened and she can't get back."

Hilde jiggled Ella in her arms. "Watch her for a moment and I'll go take a look." She put the baby down next to Dana on the bed. Ella immediately got up on her hands and knees and rocked back and forth.

"She is going to be crawling in no time," Dana said with a smile. Stacy was going to miss it. But then maybe Stacy had missed most of Ella's firsts because this wasn't her baby.

Hilde returned a few minutes later.

"You found something," Dana said, excited and worried at the same time.

"You said she didn't have much, right?" Hilde asked. "Well, she left a small duffle on the other side of the bed. Not much in it. A couple of T-shirts, underwear, socks. I searched through it." She shook her head. "Then I noticed a jean jacket hanging on the back of the chair by the window. It's not yours, is it?"

"That's the one Stacy was wearing when she arrived."

"I found this in the pocket."

Dana let out a surprised groan as Hilde, using two fingers, pulled out a small caliber handgun.

ALEX WINSLOW'S WIFE, CRYSTAL, lived up on the hill overlooking Bozeman on what some called Snob Knob. In the old days it had been called Beer Can Hill because that was where the kids used to go to drink and make out.

The house was pretty much what Liza had expected. It was huge. A contentious divorce usually meant one of three things. That the couple was fighting over the kids, the pets or the money. Since Alex and Crystal apparently had no children or pets, Liza guessed it was the money.

She parked the rental SUV Hud'd had delivered to the hospital and walked up to the massive front door. As she rang the bell, she could hear music playing inside. She rang the bell a second time before the door was opened by a petite dark-haired woman with wide blue eyes and a quizzical smile.

"Yes?" she asked.

Liza had forgotten her bandages, the eye that was turning black or that all the blood hadn't completely come out of her uniform shirt.

She'd felt there wasn't time to go all the way back to Big Sky to change. Her fear was that if she didn't solve this case soon, someone else was going to die.

"Crystal Winslow? I'm Deputy Marshal Liza Turner. I need to ask you a few questions in regard to your husband's death."

"*Estranged* husband," Crystal Winslow said, but opened the door wider. "I doubt I can be of help, but you're welcome to come in. Can I get you something?" She took in Liza's face again.

"Just answers."

Crystal led her into the formal living room. It had

a great view of the city and valley beyond. In the distance, the Spanish Peaks gleamed from the last snowfall high in the mountains.

"How long have you and Alex been estranged?"

"I don't see what that has to do—"

"Your *estranged* husband is dead. I believe whoever murdered him tried to do the same to me last night. I need to know why."

"Well, it has nothing to do with me." She sniffed, then said, "A month."

"Why?"

For a moment Crystal looked confused. "Why did I kick him out and demand a divorce? You work out of Big Sky, right? I would suggest you ask Shelby."

"Shelby Durran-Iverson?"

She nodded, and for the first time Liza saw true pain in the woman's expression—and fury. "I knew he was cheating. A woman can tell. But *Shelby?* I remember her from high school. People used to say she was the type who would eat her young."

"That could explain why she doesn't have any children," Liza said. She still felt a little lightheaded and knew this probably wasn't the best time to be interviewing anyone.

"Did Alex admit he was seeing Shelby?"

Crystal gave her an are-you-serious? look. "He swore up and down that his talking to her wasn't an affair, that he was trying to get her to tell the truth, something involving Tanner Cole."

"You remember Tanner?"

"He hung himself our senior year. I didn't really know him. He was a cowboy. I didn't date cowboys. No offense."

Liza wondered why that should offend her. Did she look that much like a cowgirl?

"I think your husband might have been telling you the truth. I believe he was looking into Tanner's death."

"Why would he do that?"

"I was hoping you could tell me since I suspect that's what got him killed."

"You don't know for sure that he wasn't having an affair with Shelby though, right?"

"No, I don't. But Alex mentioned to other people that he felt something was wrong about Tanner's suicide, as well. He didn't say anything to you?"

"No."

"Do you or your husband own any weapons?"

Crystal looked appalled. "You mean like a Saturday night special?"

"Or hunting rifles."

"No, I wouldn't have a gun in my house. My father was killed in a hunting accident. We have a state-of-the-art security system. We didn't need *guns*."

Liza nodded, knowing what that would get Crystal if someone broke into the house. She could be dead before the police arrived. "Alex didn't have weapons, either?"

"No. I still can't believe this was why Alex was spending time with Shelby."

"Did she ever call here?"

Crystal mugged a face. "Shelby said it was just to talk to Alex about Big Sky's reunion plans. They wanted their own. Ours wasn't good enough for them."

Liza could see that Crystal Winslow had been weighted down with that chip on her shoulder for some time.

"But I overheard one of his conversations," she said

smugly. "Shelby was demanding something back, apparently something she'd given him. He saw me and said he didn't know what she was talking about. After he hung up, he said Shelby was looking for some photographs from their senior year. He said she was probably using them for something she was doing for the reunion."

"You didn't believe him?"

"I could hear Shelby screeching from where I was standing. She was livid about whatever it really was."

"Did he send her some photos from high school?"

"I told you, that was just a story he came up with. He had some photographs from high school. I kept the ones of me and gave him the rest."

"Where are those photos now?"

"I threw them out with Alex. I assume he took them to his apartment," she said.

"Do you have a key?"

"He left one with me, but I've never used it." She got up and walked out of the room, returning a moment later with a shiny new key and a piece of notepaper. "Here's the address."

Liza took it. "Was that the only Big Sky friend who contacted Alex?"

"Right after that was when Alex started driving up to Big Sky and I threw him out."

"What made you suspect he was seeing Shelby?" Liza asked.

For a moment, Crystal looked confused. "I told you—"

"Right, that a woman knows. But how did you know it was *Shelby*?"

"After Tanner broke up with her in high school, she

made a play for Alex. He was dating Tessa Ryerson before that. The two of them got into it at school one day. That's when he and I started dating."

"Did he tell you what his argument with Shelby was about?"

She shrugged. "Eventually everyone has a falling-out with Shelby—except for her BFFs." She made a face, then listed off their names like a mantra. "Shelby, Tessa, Ashley, Whitney and Brittany."

Liza noted that Brittany was on the list. "When did Alex and Shelby have the falling-out?"

Crystal frowned. "It was around the time that Tanner committed suicide. After that Alex hadn't wanted anything to do with her. That is until recently."

Liza could tell that Crystal was having second thoughts about accusing her husband of infidelity.

"You said your father was killed in a hunting accident. Did you hunt?"

"No. Alex did and so did his friends," she said distractedly.

"What about Shelby?"

"She actually was a decent shot, I guess, although I suspected the only reason she and her friends hunted was to be where the boys were." Her expression turned to one of horror. "You don't think Shelby killed Alex, do you?"

Chapter Thirteen

Dana stared at the sleeping Ella as her husband updated her on Liza's condition. She'd had a scare, but she was going to be fine. In fact, she'd already checked herself out of the hospital and was working.

"You didn't try to stop her?" Dana demanded of her husband.

He gave her a look she knew too well.

"All right, what did you find out about Stacy?" she asked and braced herself for the worst.

"There is really nothing odd about her having Clay's car," she said when he finished filling her in. "Obviously they've been in contact."

"It wouldn't be odd if Clay had been cashing his checks for the last six months," Hud said. "Why would he be driving an old beater car if he had money?"

"Maybe it was a spare car he let Stacy have," she suggested.

Hud rolled his eyes. "It is the only car registered to your brother. Nice theory." He instantly seemed to regret his words. "I'm sorry. I'm not telling you these things to upset you. On the contrary, I know you'll worry more if I keep them from you."

"Which proves you're smarter than you look," she

said, annoyed that he was treating her as if she was breakable. "The babies are fine. I'm fine. You'd better not keep anything from me."

He smiled. "As I said…"

"So you can't find Clay or Stacy."

"No. But I've put an APB out on Stacy's car. It was the only thing I could do."

"Something's happened to her," Dana said. "She wouldn't leave Ella." When Hud said nothing, she shot him an impatient look. "You saw how she was with that baby. She loves her."

"Dana, we haven't seen your sister in six years. She doesn't write or call when she gets pregnant. She just shows up at the door with a baby, which she then leaves with us. Come on, even you have to admit, something is wrong with this."

She didn't want to admit it. Maybe more than anything, she didn't want to acknowledge that Stacy could have done something unforgiveable this time. Something that might land her in prison.

"What do we do now?" she asked her husband.

"I've held off going global with Ella's description, hoping Stacy would show back up. But Dana, I don't think I have any choice."

"You haven't heard anything on the DNA test you did on Ella and me?"

"I should be hearing at any time. But if the two of you aren't related, then I have to try to find out who this baby belongs to—no matter what happens to Stacy."

LIZA DROVE TO THE APARTMENT address Crystal Winslow had given her. She used the key to get into the studio apartment. As the door swung open, she caught her breath and pulled her weapon.

The apartment had been torn apart. Every conceivable hiding place had been searched, pillows and sofa bed sliced open, their stuffing spread across the room, books tossed to the floor along with clothing from the closet.

Liza listened, then cautiously stepped in. A small box of photographs had been dumped onto the floor and gone through from the looks of them. She checked the tiny kitchen and bath to make sure whoever had done this was gone before she holstered her weapon and squatted down to gingerly pick up one of the photographs.

It was a snapshot of Jordan Cardwell with two other handsome boys. All three were wearing ski clothing and looking cocky. She recognized a young Alex Winslow and assumed the other boy must be Tanner.

A curtain flapped loudly at an open window, making her start. Carefully, she glanced through the other photographs, assuming whatever the intruder had been looking for wasn't among these strewn on the floor.

It took her a moment though to realize what was missing from the pile of photos. There were none of Crystal. Nor any of Shelby or the rest of her group. That seemed odd that the women Alex had apparently been close to were missing from the old photographs. Nor were there any wedding pictures. Crystal had said she'd taken the ones of her. But who would have taken ones of Shelby and the rest of the young women he'd gone to school with in the canyon?

Rising, Liza called it in to the Bozeman Police Department, then waited until a uniformed officer arrived.

"I doubt you'll find any fingerprints, but given that Alex Winslow is a murder victim and he hasn't lived here long, I'm hoping whoever did this left us a clue," she told the officer. "I've contacted the crime lab in Missoula. I just want to make sure no one else comes in here until they arrive."

As she was leaving, Liza saw an SUV cruise slowly by. She recognized Crystal Winslow behind the wheel before the woman sped off.

JORDAN HAD JUST REACHED the bottom of the gondola for the ride up the mountain to the reunion picnic, when he spotted Liza.

She wasn't moving with her usual speed, but there was a determined look in her eye that made him smile.

"What?" she said when she joined him.

"You. After what happened, you could have taken one day off."

"I'm going to a picnic," she said. "I'm not even wearing my uniform."

She looked great out of uniform. The turquoise top she wore had slits at the shoulders, the silky fabric exposing tanned, muscled arms as it moved in the breeze. She wore khaki capris and sandals. Her long ebony-dark hair had been pulled up in back with a clip so the ends cascaded down her back. For as banged up as she was, she looked beautiful.

"I'm betting though that you're carrying a gun," he said, eyeing the leather shoulder bag hanging off one shoulder.

"You better hope I am." She laughed, but stopped quickly as if she was still light-headed.

"Are you sure you're all right?" he whispered, stepping closer.

"Dandy."

Past her, he saw Whitney and Ashley. Neither looked in a celebratory mood. When they spotted the deputy marshal, they jumped apart as if talking to each other would make them look more guilty.

"This could be a fun picnic," he said under his breath.

A few moments later Brittany arrived with her husband and small brood. Jordan was taken back again at how happy and content she looked.

I want that, he thought as his gaze shifted to Liza.

As their gondola came around, they climbed in and made room for Whitney and Ashley, who'd come up behind them. Both women, though, motioned that they would take the next one.

"I'd love to know what they're hiding," Jordan said as he sat across from the deputy marshal. The gondola door closed then rocked as it began its ascent up the mountain. He had a view of the resort and the peaks from where he sat. And a view of Liza.

He could also see the gondola below them and the two women inside. They had their heads together. He wondered at the power Shelby still held over these women she'd lorded over in high school. Did anyone ever really get over high school?

"There's something I need to ask you," Liza said, drawing his attention back to her, which was no hardship. "How was it that you were the first person on the scene last night?"

He smiled, knowing that Hud was behind this. "I got worried about you and I wanted to see you. I drove up the canyon thinking I could talk you into having dinner with me. Another car had stopped before I got there. I was just the first to go into the river." He hated that she was suspicious of him, but then again he couldn't really blame her.

"Did you see the pickup that forced me off the road?"

He nodded. "But it was just an old pickup. I was looking for your patrol SUV so I really didn't pay any attention."

She nodded. "I'd already told you I wasn't having dinner with you."

He grinned. "I thought I could charm you into changing your mind." He hurried on before she could speak. "I know you already told me no, but I thought we could at least pick up something and take it back to my cabin or your condo."

"You just don't give up, do you?"

"Kind of like someone else I know," he said and smiled at her. "I didn't have any ulterior motives. I've given this a lot of thought. Somehow, I think it all goes back to that party Tanner had at the cabin that night and the vandalism."

"And the photographs?" she asked.

He nodded. "I wish I'd stayed around long enough that night to tell you who took them."

They were almost to the top of the gondola ride. Off to his left, he saw where the caterers had set up the food for the picnic.

The gondola rocked as it came to a stop and the door opened. Jordan quickly held the doors open while the deputy marshal climbed out, then he followed, recalling what he could of that night, which wasn't much.

LIZA HOPED THE PICNIC WOULDN'T be quite as bad as the dinner had been. Jordan got them a spot near Shelby and the gang on one of the portable picnic tables that had been brought up the mountain.

"*Whatever* happened to you?" Shelby exclaimed loud enough for everyone to hear when she saw Liza.

While everyone in the canyon would have heard about her accident, Liza smiled and said, "Tripped. Sometimes I am so clumsy."

Shelby laughed. "You really should be more careful." Then she went back to holding court at her table. The usual suspects were in attendance and Tessa had been allowed to join in.

Liza watched out of the corner of her eye. Shelby monopolized the conversation with overly cheerful banter. But it was as if a pall had fallen over her group that not even she could lift.

After they ate, some of the picnickers played games in the open area next to the ski lift. When Liza spotted Tessa heading for the portable toilets set up in the trees, she excused herself and followed.

Music drifted on the breeze. A cloudless blue sky hung over Lone Peak. It really was the perfect day for a picnic and she said as much to Tessa when she caught up with her.

"Deputy," Tessa said.

"Why don't you call me Liza."

The woman smiled. "So I forget that I'm talking to the *law?*"

"I'm here as Jordan Cardwell's date."

Tessa chuckled at that, then sobered. "What happened to you?"

"Someone tried to stop me from looking into Alex's and Tanner's deaths."

The woman let out a groan.

"I was hoping you would have contacted me to talk," Liza said. "I can see you're troubled."

"Troubled?" Tessa laughed as she glanced back toward the group gathered below them on the mountain.

Liza followed her gaze and saw Shelby watching them. "We should step around the other side."

Tessa didn't argue. As they moved out of Shelby's sight, Tessa stopped abruptly and reached into her shoulder bag. "Here," she said, thrusting an envelope at the deputy marshal. "Alex left it with me and told me not to show it to anyone. He said to just keep it and not look inside until I had to."

Liza saw that it was sealed. "You didn't look?"

Tessa shook her head quickly.

"What did he mean, 'until you had to'?"

"I have no idea. I don't know what's in there and I don't care. If anyone even found out I had it…"

"Why did he trust *you* with this?" Liza had to ask.

Tessa looked as if she wasn't going to answer, then seemed to figure there was no reason to lie anymore. "I was in love with him. I have been since high school. Shelby always told me he wasn't good enough for me." She began to cry, but quickly wiped her eyes at the sound of someone moving through the dried grass on the other side of the portable toilets.

Liza hurriedly stuffed the envelope into her own shoulder bag.

An instant later Shelby came around the end of the stalls. "Are they all occupied?" she asked, taking in the two of them, then glancing toward the restrooms.

"I just used that one," Liza improvised. She turned and started back down the hillside.

Behind her she heard Shelby ask Tessa, "What did she want?"

She didn't hear Tessa's answer, but she feared Shelby wouldn't believe anything her friend said anyway. Tessa was running scared and anyone could see it—especially Shelby, who had her own reasons for being afraid.

Liza thought about the manila envelope Alex had left in Tessa's safekeeping. What was inside it? The photographs that Shelby had been trying to get her hands on? Liza couldn't wait to find out.

HUD HAD PUT A RUSH ON ELLA'S relational DNA test. He'd done it for Dana's sake. He saw that by the hour she was getting more attached to that baby. If he was right and Stacy had kidnapped it, then Dana's heart was going to be broken.

He was as anxious as she was to get the results. Meanwhile he needed to search for Stacy as he continued to watch for possible kidnappings on the law enforcement networks.

So far, he'd come up with nothing.

He found himself worrying not only about Stacy's disappearance, but also everything else that was going on. He'd done his best to stay out of Liza's hair. She could handle the murder case without him, he kept telling himself. Still, he'd been glad when Hilde had called and said she could come stay with Dana if he needed her to.

His phone rang as he paced in the living room. He'd never been good at waiting. He saw on caller ID that it was Shelby Durran-Iverson.

"Marshal Savage," he answered and listened while Shelby complained about Liza. It seemed she'd seen the deputy kissing Jordan. Hud swore silently. He had warned Liza about Jordan, but clearly she hadn't listened.

"Deputies get to have private lives," he told Shelby.

"Really? Even with the man who was with Alex when he was murdered? I would think Jordan Cardwell is a suspect. Or at least should be."

It was taking all his self-control to keep from telling Shelby that she was more of a suspect than Jordan was.

"I'll look into it," he said.

"I should hope you'd do more than that. Isn't fraternizing with a suspect a violation that could call for at least a suspension—if not dismissal?"

"I said I would look into it." He hung up just as a car pulled up in front of the house. With a sigh of relief, he started to open the door to greet Hilde when he saw that it wasn't her car. Nor was it Stacy's.

When he saw who climbed out, he let out a curse. Before he could answer the door, his phone rang again. Figuring to get all the bad news over with quickly, he took the call from the lab as he heard footfalls on the porch and a tentative knock at the door.

"Hud, who is that at the door?" Dana called.

He listened to the lab tech give him the news, then thanked him and, disconnecting, stepped to her bedroom doorway.

"What is it?" she demanded. "Was that the lab on the phone?"

He nodded. "Ella *is* your niece."

Dana began to cry and laugh at the same time as she looked into Ella's beautiful face.

There was another knock at the door.

"Is that Stacy?" she asked, looking up, her eyes full of hope.

He shook his head. "I wish," he said and went to answer the door.

Chapter Fourteen

"Clay?" Dana said as her younger brother appeared in the bedroom doorway, Jordan at his heels.

"Hi," he said shyly. Clay had always been the quiet one, the one who ducked for cover when the rest of them were fighting. "Jordan told me you're pregnant with twins. Congratulations."

"Jordan?" she asked, shooting a look at her older brother. "Clay, what are you doing here?"

"I called Clay at the studio where I knew he was working," Jordan said.

"The studio let me use the company plane, so here I am," Clay said.

"Tell me what is going on. Why haven't you cashed your checks for the past six months and why does Stacy have your car?"

"Easy," Hud said as he stepped into the room. He gave both her brothers a warning look.

She didn't look at her husband. Her gaze was on her younger brother.

"I've been in Europe the past six months, then I changed apartments and forgot to put in a change of address," Clay said. "That's why I haven't cashed my checks. As for the car, I wasn't using it, so I told Stacy she could have it. I'm working for a movie studio in L.A. so I have a studio car that picks me up every morning."

"I'm glad things are going well for you," Dana said. "But you know what's going on with Stacy, don't you?"

"All I know is that she said she needed to get here to the ranch and could she borrow my car," Clay said. "So where is she?"

"That is the question," Hud said next to him. "She seems to have disappeared."

"Well, if you're worried because she has my car, it's no big deal."

"It's not the car that we're worried about," Dana said. "She left her baby here."

"Her *baby?*" Clay said. "Stacy has a baby?"

At the sound of another vehicle, Hud quickly left the room. Dana assumed it would be Hilde, but when he returned, he had Liza with him.

"You've met my brother Clay," Dana said.

Liza nodded. "Looks like you're having a family reunion."

"Doesn't it though," Hud said under his breath.

"Yes, all we need is Stacy," Dana said. "And a larger bedroom." She saw a look pass between the deputy and her husband. "I know that look. What's happened?"

"I just need to talk to the marshal for a few moments," Liza said. "But I'm going to need Jordan." He nodded and stepped out of the room with her and Hud, closing the door behind them.

"I can't stand being in this bed and not knowing what's going on," Dana said.

Clay was looking at the baby lying next to her. "Is that Stacy's?"

"Yes," Dana said with a sigh as Ella stirred awake.

At least Stacy hadn't kidnapped Ella. This little baby was Dana's niece. But where was Stacy? And did whatever Liza needed to talk to Hud and Jordan about have something to do with her sister or the murder?

"I THINK YOU'D BETTER SEE these photographs," Liza said to Hud the moment the bedroom door closed behind him. "Tessa gave them to me. She said Alex had left them in her safekeeping."

"Alex *trusted* Tessa?" Jordan said. "He had to know how close she was to Shelby."

"Obviously Alex trusted her not to give the photos to Shelby," Hud said and gave Jordan a how-did-you-get-involved-in-this-discussion? look.

"Tessa and Alex had a history," Liza said and told them what Crystal Winslow had told her. "She thought Alex was having an affair with Shelby, but I think it might have been Tessa. The two of them were dating in high school when Shelby broke them up so Tessa could spy on Tanner, right, Jordan?" He nodded and she continued. "That's a bond that Alex and Tessa shared against Shelby. With Tessa's marriage over and Alex's apparently not going well, they reconnected."

Hud looked through the photos then reluctantly handed them to Jordan. "You know the people in the photos?" he asked his brother-in-law.

Jordan nodded. "So someone took photos of the party. This can't be enough to get Alex killed over."

She waited until Jordan had finished going through the photos before she took them back, sorted through them until she found the two she wanted, then produced a magnifying glass from her pocket. "Check this out."

They all moved over to the table as Liza put the large

magnifying glass over the first photograph. "You can clearly see Malcolm Iverson's construction equipment in the background. But look here." She pointed at a spot to the left of one of the large dump trucks.

Jordan let out a surprised, "Whoa. It's Shelby."

Liza moved the magnifying glass to the second photo and both men took a look.

"Shelby vandalized the equipment," Jordan said. He let out a low whistle and looked at Liza. "You can clearly see Shelby dressed in black, dumping sugar into one of the two-ton trucks' gas tanks. If these photographs would have come out back then, she could have gone to jail."

Liza nodded. "Shelby has every reason in the world not to want these photographs to ever see daylight. She's married to the man whose father she bankrupted by vandalizing his construction equipment. The rest is like knocking over dominos. She vandalizes the equipment, Malcolm Iverson blames Harris Lancaster and shoots him, Malcolm goes to prison, then gets out and mysteriously dies in a boating accident."

"She didn't pull this off alone," Jordan said.

"No," Liza agreed. "In these two photos you can see Whitney and Ashley are keeping everyone's attention on them at the campfire," she said as she showed them two other photographs of the girls pretending to strip to whatever music was playing.

"Where was Tessa?" Jordan asked.

"With Tanner in the woods," Liza said and sifted through the photos until she found one of Tanner and Tessa coming out of the woods together.

Jordan let out a low whistle. "Shelby thought of everything."

"She just didn't realize that someone was taking photographs of the party," Liza said.

"I wonder where the negatives are. Alex wasn't dumb enough to trust Tessa completely. So who has the negatives?"

"Jordan has a point," Liza said.

Hud looked at his brother-in-law. "You should have gone into law enforcement."

Jordan smiled. "I'm going to take that as a compliment."

"I'm sure Hud meant it as one," Liza said.

"If Alex had the goods on Shelby and was blackmailing her, then why ask around about photos that were already in his possession? Or hint that Tanner's death wasn't a suicide?" Hud asked.

"Maybe he just wanted to shake up those involved. Or shake them down. What I'd like to know is who took the photos," Jordan said.

She looked over at him. "I just assumed Alex did since he isn't in any of them. Was he at the party that night?"

Jordan shrugged. "He was earlier."

"So these could merely be copies of photographs taken at the party," Hud said. "Which means there could be more than one person shopping the photos. That is what you're getting at, right, Deputy? Blackmail? For the past twenty years?"

Liza shook her head. "At least Alex hasn't been blackmailing Shelby for twenty years that I can find. I got his bank records for the past two years faxed to me. He made his first deposits only four months ago. Nine thousand dollars each month. He must have known that anything over ten thousand dollars would be red flagged by the bank."

"Why wait twenty years if he was going to black-mail Shelby?" Hud asked.

"I suspect that when his wife threw him out—along with all his stuff including some old photographs from high school, he hadn't looked at them in years," Liza said. "When he did, he saw what we're seeing and, since he already had reason to hate Shelby over the Tessa deal, decided to blackmail her."

"And she killed him," Jordan said.

Hud sighed. "Can we prove it?"

"Not yet," Liza said as she sorted through the pho-tographs. "But I overheard Shelby on the phone with a creditor saying the check was in the mail. I asked around. Yogamotion has been having trouble paying its bills the past few months, but Hilde says it is packed for every class and it isn't cheap to join."

"So have you talked to Shelby yet?" Hud asked.

She shook her head. "There's something else you need to see." She pointed to a figure in the shadows of the pines at the edge of the campfire in one of the photographs.

"Stacy?" Hud said after taking the photo from her and using the magnifying glass to bring his sister-in-law's face into focus. He groaned and looked at Jordan.

"She wasn't there when I left," he said, holding up his hands. "It never dawned on me that she might have been at the party. We never went to the same parties or hung with the same crowd, so I have no idea what she was doing there."

"This could explain why Stacy came back to the can-yon," Hud said with a curse.

"Maybe it is just bad timing on her part." Liza tapped

the photo. "But Stacy knows who was taking the photographs. She's looking right at the person with the camera."

"Which means she also knew there were photographs taken of the party that night."

"HUD?"

"Dana, what is it?" he cried, hearing something in his wife's voice that scared him. He rushed to the bedroom door to find Clay holding Dana's hand. Ella was crying.

"Can you take Ella? She needs a bottle," Dana said.

He tried to calm down. "That's all?" Then he saw his wife grimace. "What was that?" he demanded as Liza volunteered to take the crying baby and get Ella a bottle. Jordan had moved to the side of Dana's bed.

"A twinge. I've been having them all day," Dana admitted.

"Why didn't you tell me?" he demanded.

"Because I didn't want to worry you." She cringed as she had another one, this one definitely stronger from her reaction.

"I'm calling the doctor," he said and started to turn from the crowded room.

Hud hadn't heard a car drive up let alone anyone else enter the house so he was surprised to turn and see Stacy standing in the doorway of Dana's bedroom.

Maybe more shocking was how bad she looked. Both eyes were black and the blood from a cut on her cheek had dried to a dark red. Her hair was matted to her head on one side with what Hud guessed was also blood.

Dana let out a startled cry when she saw her sister.

"I wasn't completely honest with you," Stacy said in a hoarse voice as she stumbled forward.

That's when Hud saw the man behind her, the one holding the gun.

"Just get the baby," the man ordered Stacy, jabbing her in the back with the barrel of the gun. "Then we won't be troubling you people any further."

Stacy moved toward the bassinet that had been brought in next to Dana's bed. She leaned over it, gripping the sides.

Hud saw the bruises on her neck and noticed the way she was favoring her left side as if her ribs hurt her. He looked at the man in the doorway still holding the gun on Stacy.

"What's this about?" he asked the man, trying to keep his tone calm while his heart was pounding. Dana was in labor. He needed to get her to the hospital. He didn't need whatever trouble Stacy was in right now.

"Didn't Stacy tell you? She made off with my kid."

"She's my baby, too, Virgil," Stacy said, still staring down into the crib.

Hud remembered that the crib was empty because Liza had taken the baby into the kitchen with her to get her a bottle.

"He took Ella away from me," Stacy said, crying.

"Her name isn't *Ella*," Virgil snapped. "I told you I was naming her after my mother. Her name is Katie, you stupid b—"

"He took her from me right after she was born and has been raising her with his girlfriend," Stacy said through her tears. "He would only let me come see her a few times."

"Because you'd make a crappy mother. Letting you even see her was a mistake," the man spat. "Now get the damned baby and let's go."

Even the thought of this man taking Ella made Hud

sick to his stomach. But he couldn't have any gunplay around Dana, especially since his own gun was locked up like it always was when he was home with the kids.

Dana still kept a shotgun by the kitchen back door though, high on the wall where the kids couldn't reach it, but handy for adults. He wondered if Liza had heard Stacy and the man come in, if she had any idea what was going on?

Stacy turned her head, her gaze locking with Hud's, as she pleaded for his help.

"Let me get the baby for you," Hud said and stepped to the bassinet.

LIZA HAD BEEN HEATING A BOTTLE of formula for Ella when she heard the door open, then close softly. She listened, drawn by the faint sound of footfalls crossing the living room to Dana's door.

She peered around the corner in time to see the man with the gun. Her heart leaped to her throat. She was out of uniform, her weapon was in the car and she had a baby in one arm. She carefully opened the door of the microwave before it could ding and looked at Ella. The baby grinned at her and flapped her arms.

"I'm going to have to put you down. I need you to be really quiet," Liza whispered. She looked around for a place to put the baby and decided the rug in front of the sink was going to have to do. Carefully, she put down the baby. As she was rising, she saw the shotgun hanging high on the wall over the back door.

Knowing Dana, the shotgun would be loaded. All she could do was pray that it was since she wouldn't have the first idea where to look for shells. She could hear Ella babbling on the rug behind her and trying to snake toward her.

Hurry. She reached up on tiptoes and eased the shotgun off its rack. Trying not to make a sound, she cracked the gun open. Two shells. She dearly loved Dana who knew there was nothing more worthless than an unloaded shotgun.

Ella was watching her expectantly as she crept to the kitchen doorway. She could see the man with the gun, but she could hear voices coming from Dana's bedroom. Normally, she was cool and calm. It was what made her a good cop. But so much was riding on what she did now, she felt the weight of it at heart level.

She had no idea what she would be walking into. No idea who the man was or why he was in this house with a gun. Moving along the edge of the room to keep the old hardwood floor from creaking, she headed for the bedroom doorway.

"Come on, hurry it up. Give me the baby," snapped a male voice she didn't recognize. "We don't have all day."

Liza was next to the doorway. She could see the man holding the gun. He had it pointed at Stacy who was standing next to Hud beside the empty bassinet. Hud had his hands inside the bassinet. He appeared to be rolling up Ella's quilt.

Taking a breath, she let it out slowly, the same way she did at the gun range just before she shot.

Then she moved quickly. She jammed the barrel of shotgun into the man's side and in clear, loud voice said, "Drop the gun or I will blow a hole in you the size of Montana."

The man froze for a moment, then slowly turned his

head to look at her. When he saw her, he smiled. "Put down the shotgun before you hurt yourself, little lady."

"There's something I wasn't honest with you about either," Stacy said turning from the bassinet. "My brother-in-law is a marshal and that woman holding a shotgun is a deputy. She will kill you if you don't drop your gun."

"But I'll kill you first," he snarled and lifted the gun to take aim.

Liza moved in quickly, slamming the barrel hard into his ribs as Hud threw Stacy to the floor. Her momentum drove the man back and into the wall. She knocked the pistol from his hand, then cold-cocked him with the shotgun. As his eyes rolled back into his head, he slid down the wall to the floor.

Hud already had the man's gun and bent to frisk him, pulling out his wallet. "Dana, are you all right?" he asked over his shoulder. Liza could hear Stacy sobbing.

"I'm fine," Dana said.

The marshal rose. "I'll get my cuffs." He was back an instant later and had the man cuffed. Liza hadn't taken her eyes off their prisoner. She'd seen his hand twitch and knew he was coming around.

"Stacy, Ella is in the kitchen on the floor," Liza said over her shoulder.

"I'm not leaving without my baby," the man screamed at Stacy as she hurried past her and into the kitchen. "I'll kill you next time. I swear, I'm going to kill you."

Hud hauled him to his feet. "You aren't going anywhere but jail. You just threatened to kill my sister-in-law in front of a half dozen witnesses."

"I'll take him in," Liza said. "You take Dana to the hospital. I heard her say her water just broke." As she led him out of the house, Liza began to read him his rights.

Chapter Fifteen

After booking Virgil Browning, Liza was just in time to catch Shelby as she was coming out of Yogamotion. She had a large bag, the handles looped over one shoulder, and seemed to be in a hurry. As Liza had walked past Shelby's SUV, she'd noticed there were suitcases in the back.

"I'm sorry, we're closed, Deputy," Shelby said. "And I'm in a hurry."

"You might want to open back up. Unless you want to discuss why you were being blackmailed at your house with your husband present."

All the color washed from the woman's face. She leaned into the door as if needing it for support. "I don't—"

"Don't bother lying. Alex would have bled you dry since his wife was taking everything in the divorce, right? He needed money and he had you right where he wanted you. *Of course,* you had to kill him."

"I didn't kill Alex." When Liza said nothing, Shelby opened the door to Yogamotion and turned on the light as they both stepped back inside.

Liza saw the sign that had been taped to the door.

Closed Until Further Notice. Shelby was skipping town, sure as the devil.

"I swear I didn't kill him," she said as they went into her office and sat down. "Why would I kill him? I had no idea who was blackmailing me," Shelby cried.

Liza studied her face for a moment, trying to decide if she was telling the truth or lying through her teeth.

"So how was it you made the payment if you didn't know who was blackmailing you?"

"I sent ten thousand dollars in cash to J. Doe, general delivery in Bozeman each month."

"You were that afraid of the truth coming out?" Liza had to ask.

"How can you ask that?" Shelby cried. "It wasn't just the vandalism. Wyatt's father lost his business, went to prison and probably killed himself, all because of what I did." She was crying now, real tears.

"You had to know it would eventually come out."

She shook her head adamantly. "It would destroy my marriage, my reputation, I'd have to leave town. Wyatt has said if he ever found out who did that to his father, he'd kill them."

Liza felt a chill run the length of her spine. "Maybe he's already killed. Didn't he blame Tanner for what happened?"

She quit crying for a moment and wiped at her tears, frowning as she realized what Liza was saying. "Yes, he blamed Tanner, but he wouldn't..." The words died off. "Tanner killed *himself.*"

"Did he? Was Wyatt jealous of your relationship with Tanner?" Liza saw the answer in the woman's expression. "Tanner was supposed to be watching the equipment, right?"

"No, Wyatt wouldn't…" She shook her head. "He's had to overcome so much."

"Does he know about the blackmail?"

"No, of course not."

But Liza could see the fear in the woman's eyes. "If he found out that you were being blackmailed and thought it was Alex Winslow behind it, what would your husband do?"

"He couldn't have found out," she said. "If he knew, he would have left me."

Liza thought about that for a moment. "What if you weren't the only one being blackmailed?"

Shelby's head came up. "What?"

"Has your husband been having similar financial problems to yours?" Liza asked.

"It's the economy," Shelby said. "It's not…"

"Because he's been paying a blackmailer just like you have?"

"Why would he do that?" Her eyes widened and Liza saw that, like her, Shelby could think of only one reason her husband might be paying a blackmailer.

"Oh, no, no." She began to wail, a high keening sound. "He wouldn't have hurt Tanner. Not Tanner." She rocked back and forth, hugging her stomach.

"I have to ask you," Liza said. "Were you ever pregnant with Tanner's baby?"

Her wailing didn't stop, but it slowed. She shook her head, before she dropped it into her hands. "I didn't want him to leave Big Sky after graduation. I thought that if he married me I could say I had a miscarriage. Or with luck, I could get pregnant quickly."

"Where is your husband?" Liza asked her.

"He's been out of town, but I expect him back tonight."

"That's why you were leaving. You're afraid your husband has found out."

Shelby didn't have to answer. The terror in her eyes said it all.

"I'd tell you not to leave town," Liza said, "but I'm afraid that advice could get you killed tonight."

Shelby's cell phone rang. She glanced at it. "I need to take this."

As Liza was walking away, she heard Shelby say, "I'm so sorry." She was crying, her last words garbled but still intelligible. "Really? Just give me a few minutes."

AFTER LEAVING THE RANCH, Jordan drove around aimlessly. His mind whirled with everything that had happened since his return to the canyon.

Foremost was Alex and Liza's blackmail theory. Alex had always resented the rich people who came and went at Big Sky—but especially those who built the huge houses they lived in only a few weeks each year.

So had Alex blackmailed Shelby for the money? Or for breaking him and Tessa up all those years ago?

But was that what had gotten him killed? As much as he disliked Shelby, he couldn't imagine her actually shooting Alex. True she used to hunt, maybe still did, and hadn't been a bad shot. And she was cold-blooded, no doubt about that.

It just felt as if there had to be more.

Both Hud and Liza had warned him to leave town and stay out of the investigation. He couldn't, even if he wanted to. Driving past Yogamotion, he saw that the lights were out. There was a note on the door. Getting out, he walked to the door. Closed Until Further Notice.

He pulled out his cell phone and tried Shelby's house. No answer. Then he got Crystal Winslow's number from information and waited for her to pick up.

"Hello?"

"Crystal, you probably don't remember me, I'm Jordan Cardwell."

"I remember you." Her voice sounded laced with ice.

"I need to ask you something about Alex. I heard he majored in engineering at Montana State University. Is that how he made his money?"

"He was a consultant. He worked for large construction projects like bridges and highways and some smaller ones that I am only now finding out about."

He heard something in her voice, a bitterness. "Smaller jobs?"

"Apparently, he was working for Shelby Iverson and had been for years. Her husband signed the checks, but I'm betting she was behind it. He must have thought I was so stupid. What could Iverson Construction need an engineer consultant for? They build houses."

"Crystal, how often did they hire Alex?"

"Every month for years."

"Twenty years?"

"All these years." She was crying. "That bitch has been…playing my husband like a puppet on the string."

More likely it was Alex playing her. So he had been blackmailing not Shelby, but Wyatt since Tanner's death and hiding it as work-related payments. No wonder Liza hadn't found it.

As he told Crystal how sorry he was and hung up, he wondered how Wyatt had been able to hide this from

Shelby all these years. With building going crazy at Big Sky until recently, maybe it hadn't been that much of a strain on Wyatt.

He would ask Wyatt when he saw him. Which would be soon, he thought as he parked in front of the Iverson mansion on the hill. The place looked deserted. As he started to get out a big black SUV came roaring up.

WYATT IVERSON LOOKED HARRIED and dirty as if he'd just been working at one of his construction sites. He had a cut on his cheek that the blood had only recently dried on and bruises as if he'd been in a fist fight. "If you're looking for Shelby, she's not here."

"Actually, I was looking for you," Jordan said, not caring what had happened to Wyatt Iverson or his wife. "Have a minute?"

"No, I just got home. I've been out of town."

"This won't take long," Jordan said, following him up the steps to the front door and pushing past him into the large marble foyer. "I just need to know how you killed Tanner Cole. I already suspect *why* you did it, misguided as it was." Through an open doorway he saw a large bedroom with women's clothing strewn all over the bed and floor. Shelby either had trouble finding something to wear tonight or she had hightailed it out of town.

"I really don't have time for this," Wyatt said behind him.

He got as far as the living room with its white furniture he would bet no one had ever sat on, before he turned to look into the other man's face. Wyatt was magazine-model handsome, a big, muscled man, but Jordan was sure he could take him in a fair fight.

Unfortunately, when he saw the gun in Wyatt Iverson's hand, he knew he wasn't going to get a chance to find out.

"You want to know how your friend died?" Wyatt demanded. "I told him that everything was going to be all right. That he shouldn't blame himself for my father's construction equipment being vandalized. He'd already had a few drinks by the time I got to the cabin." Wyatt stopped just inches from Jordan now.

"Tanner felt horrible about what had happened, blamed himself," he continued, a smirk on his face. "I suggested we have more drinks and bury the hatchet so to speak. By the time we went out by the fire pit, he was feeling no pain. I kept plying him with booze until he could barely stand up, then I bet him he couldn't balance on an upturned log. You should have seen his expression when I put the noose around his neck."

Jordan knew the worst thing he could do was go for the gun. Wyatt had the barrel aimed at his heart and, from the trapped look in the man's eyes, he would use it if provoked. But seeing that Wyatt Iverson felt no remorse for what he'd done and realizing the man was ready to kill again, Jordan lunged at the gun.

Wyatt was stronger than he looked and clearly he'd been expecting—probably hoping—Jordan would try something. The sound of the gunshot ricocheted through the expanse of the large living room, a deafening report that was followed by a piercing pain in Jordan's shoulder.

Wyatt twisted the gun from his fingers and backhanded him with the butt. Jordan saw stars and suddenly the room started spinning. The next thing he knew he was on the floor, looking up at the man. His shoulder hurt like hell, but the bullet appeared to have only grazed his skin.

"You lousy bastard." Jordan struggled to get up, but Wyatt kicked him hard in the stomach, then knelt down beside him, holding the gun to his head.

"Your friend knew he deserved it. I told him how my old man had let his insurance on the equipment lapse, how this would destroy my family and your friend Tanner nodded and closed his eyes and I kicked the log out."

"You *murdered* him," Jordan said between clenched teeth.

"He got what he deserved."

"He didn't deserve to die because of some vandalized equipment even if he had been responsible. Shelby set up Tanner that night—from the party to the vandalism—to get back at him. It was that old story of a woman scorned."

With a start Jordan saw that this wasn't news. Wyatt had known. "How long have you known that you killed the wrong person? Then you killed Alex to keep it your little family secret and end the blackmail?"

"*Alex?* I didn't kill Alex."

Jordan started to call the man a liar. But why would he lie at a time like this when he'd already confessed to one murder? With a jolt, Jordan realized that Wyatt was telling the truth. He didn't kill Alex. *Shelby.* No wonder she'd taken off. Not only would it now come out about her vandalizing the Iverson Construction equipment, but that she'd killed Alex to keep the photographs from going public.

"Where's your wife, Iverson?" Jordan asked through the pain as Wyatt jerked him to his feet and dragged him toward the front door with the gun to his head.

"Have you known all along it was her? No? Then you must be furious. Did you catch her packing to make her getaway?" Jordan had a thought. "Does she know that you killed Tanner?"

Wyatt made a sound that sent a chill up Jordan's spine.

He thought about the cut and bruise on Iverson's cheek, that harried look in his eye—and the dirt on him as if he'd been digging at one of his construction sites. "What did you do to her?" he demanded. "You wouldn't kill your own wife!"

"One more word and I'll kill you right there," the man said as he pulled him outside to the rental car. He reached inside and released the latch on the hatchback.

"You're going to kill me anyway. But you have to know you can't get away with this." He felt the shove toward the open back of the SUV just an instant before the blow to his head. Everything went dark. His last clear thought was of Tanner and what he must have felt the moment Wyatt kicked the log out from under his feet.

Liza called Hud's cell on her way to the Iverson house.

"How is Dana?" she asked first.

"In labor. We're at the hospital and they are making her comfortable. They're talking C-section, but you know Dana. She's determined she's going to have these babies the natural way."

"Give her my best. Did you get a chance to ask Stacy about Tanner's party?" she asked as she drove toward the mountain and the Iverson house.

"She was pretty shaken up after what happened and I got busy, but she's standing right here. I'll let you talk to her since I have to get back to Dana." He handed off the phone.

A moment later a shaky-voiced Stacy said, "Hello?"

"I need to know about the party Tanner Cole had at the Iverson Construction site twenty years ago."

"What?"

"You were there. I've seen a photograph of you standing around the campfire. I need to know who shot the photos. Come on, Stacy, it wasn't that long after that that Tanner died. Don't tell me you don't remember."

"I remember," she said, sounding defensive. "I was just trying to understand why you would ask me who took the photos. I did. It was my camera."

"*Your* camera? Why were you taking photographs at the party?"

"Jordan. I wanted to get something on him," she said. "He was always telling on me to Mother."

Blackmail, great. Liza sighed. "If it was your camera, then how is it that there's a photo of you?"

Silence then. "Alex Winslow. He wanted to borrow the camera for a moment. I made him give it back—"

"By promising to get him copies," Liza finished.

"Yes, how did you—"

"Do you still have the negatives?"

"I doubt it. Unless they're stored in my things I left here at the ranch."

"Let me talk to Jordan," Liza said, feeling as if all the pieces of the puzzle were finally coming together.

"Jordan? He's not here. He asked me who took the photos, then he left, saying he'd come by the hospital later."

"Do you know where he went?" Liza asked, suddenly worried.

"He said something about blackmail and the other side of the coin."

Ahead, Liza saw the Iverson house come into view in her headlights. "If you see him, tell him to call my cell." She gave Stacy the number, then disconnected as she pulled into the wide paved drive.

Parking, she tried Jordan's cell phone number. It went straight to voice mail. She left a message for him to call her.

The Iverson house could only be described as a mansion. But then Wyatt Iverson was in the construction business. Of course his home would have to be magnificent.

Liza got out and walked up the steps to the wide veranda. She rang the doorbell, heard classical music play inside and was reminded of Crystal Winslow's house down in Bozeman. It wasn't anywhere as large or as grand.

Liza thought about an old Elvis Presley song about a house without love. Or honesty, she thought as she rang the bell again.

Getting no answer, she checked the five-car garage. There was a large ski boat, a trailer with four snowmobiles and the large black SUV, the same one Liza had seen Wyatt Iverson driving the night of the reunion dinner.

He'd returned home. So where was he? And where was Jordan? She tried his cell phone again. As before, it went straight to voice mail.

Something was wrong. She felt it in her bones. If Wyatt Iverson had returned, where else might he have gone? She recalled overhearing Shelby say what sounded like she was going to meet someone. Was she stupid enough to agree to see her husband? If so, where would they have gone if not their house?

Yogamotion was her first thought. But she'd seen Shelby hightail it out of there. Was it possible Wyatt had taken another vehicle? She thought about Jordan. What if he'd come up here as she suspected?

She didn't want to go down that particular trail of thought. Maybe Wyatt Iverson had gone by his construction office. Unlike his father, Wyatt kept all his equipment under lock and key at a site back up Moonlight Basin.

She hurried to her rental SUV and, climbing behind the wheel, started the engine and headed for Moonlight Basin. All her instincts told her to hurry.

Chapter Sixteen

Jordan came to in darkness. He blinked, instantly aware of the pain. His wrists were bound with duct tape behind him. More duct tape bound his ankles. A strip had been placed over his mouth. He lay in the back of the rented SUV. Outside the vehicle he heard a sound he recognized and sat up, his head swimming. Something warm and sticky ran down into his left eye. Blood.

Through the blood he looked out through an array of construction equipment. He couldn't see the piece of equipment that was making all the noise, but he could see a gravel pit behind the site and catch movement.

Now seemed an odd time to be digging in a gravel pit. Unless, he thought with a start, you wanted to bury something.

Jordan knew he was lucky to be alive. He'd been a damned fool going to Iverson's house unarmed. What had he hoped to accomplish? The answer was simple. He'd wanted to hear Wyatt Iverson admit to Tanner's murder. He'd also wanted to know how he'd done it.

So he'd accomplished what he'd set out to do—a suicidal mission that had been successful if one didn't take his current predicament into consideration.

Hurriedly, he began to work at the tape on his wrists.

There were few sharp edges in the back of the SUV. Nor could he get the door open thanks to child locks. In frustration at modern advances, he threw himself into the backseat and was headed for the front seat to unlock the doors, when he heard it.

The noise of the running equipment had dropped to a low purr.

Jordan felt around quickly for a sharp edge. He found it on the metal runner of the front passenger seat and began to work frantically at the tape. Whatever Wyatt Iverson had been up to, he'd stopped. Jordan had a bad feeling that he'd be coming for him any moment.

The tape gave way. He quickly peeled the strip from his mouth then reached down to free his ankles.

The back door of the SUV swung open and he was instantly blinded by the glaring beam of a heavy-duty flashlight.

"Get out," Iverson barked.

Jordan saw that the gun was in the man's other hand and the barrel was pointed at him. He freed his ankles and did as he was told. As he stepped out, he breathed in the cold night air. It made him shiver. Or it could have been the sudden knowledge of what Iverson planned to do with him.

Standing, he could see where the earth had been dug out in a long trench. There was already one vehicle at the bottom of the trench. He recognized Shelby's expensive SUV.

"Get behind the wheel," Iverson ordered, and holding the gun on him, climbed in behind him in the backseat.

Jordan could feel the cold hard metal of the gun barrel pressed against his neck.

"Start the car." Iverson tossed him the keys.

His hand was shaking as he inserted the key. The engine turned right over even though he was wishing for a dead battery right then.

"Now drive through the gate to the back of the property. Try anything and I'll put a bullet into your brain and jump out."

Jordan drove through the gate and down the path that led to the gravel pit and ultimately the trench Iverson had dug for Shelby—and now him. He realized there was only one thing he could do. Iverson would have him stop at the high end of the trench. He would get out and send Jordan to his death—either before he buried him at the bottom of the trench or after.

He hit the child locks so Iverson couldn't get out and gunned the engine. He would take Iverson with him, one way or the other.

As the Iverson Construction site came into view, Liza noticed that the large metal gate hung open. She cut her headlights and slowly pulled to the side of the road.

It wasn't until she shut off her engine and got out that she heard the sound of a front-end loader running in the distance. Drawing her weapon, she moved through the darkness toward the sound.

She'd just cleared the fence and most of the equipment when she saw an old red pickup parked back between some other old trucks. She could see where the right side of it was all banged up. Some of the paint of the patrol SUV was still on the side. It was definitely the pickup that had run her off the road.

Ahead she heard a car start up. She could make out movement in the faint starlight. She hurried toward it, keeping to the shadows so she wasn't spotted.

But the car didn't come in her direction as she'd thought it would. Instead, it went the other way. In its headlights she saw the gravel pit and finally the trench and the front-end loader idling nearby.

To her amazement the vehicle engine suddenly roared. The driver headed for the trench.

Liza ran through the darkness, her heart hammering, as the vehicle careened down the slope and into the narrow ditch. She reached the fence, rushed through the gate and across the flat area next to the gravel pit in time to see the lights of the vehicle disappear into the trench.

Her mind was racing. What in the—

The sound of metal meeting metal filled the night air. She came to a skidding stop at the edge of the trough and looked down to see two vehicles. Smoke rose from between their crumpled metal, the headlights of the second one dimmed by the dirt and gravel that had fallen down around it.

She waited a moment for the driver to get out, then realizing he must be trapped in there, the trench too narrow for him to open his door, she scrambled down into the deep gully, weapon ready.

As she neared the vehicle, she recognized it. The rental SUV Jordan had been driving. Her pulse began to pound. Jordan did crazy things sometimes, she thought, remembering how he'd swum out into the river to be with her while she waited for the ambulance to arrive.

But he wouldn't purposely drive into this trench, would he? Which begged the question, where was Wyatt Iverson?

"COME ON, BABIES," DANA SAID under her breath and pushed.

"That's it," her doctor said. "Almost there. Just one more push."

Dana closed her eyes. She could feel Hud gripping her hand. Her first twin was about to make his or her way into the world. She felt the contraction, hard and fast, and pushed.

"It's a boy!" A cheer came up at the end of the bed. She opened her eyes and looked into the mirror positioned over the bed as the doctor held up her baby.

A moment later she heard the small, high-pitched cry of her son and tried to relax as Hud whispered that they had a perfect baby boy.

Dr. Burr placed the baby in Dana's arms for a moment. She smiled down at the crinkled adorable face before the doctor handed the baby off to the nurses standing by. "One more now. Let's see how that one's doing."

Dana could hear the baby's strong heartbeat through the monitor. She watched the doctor's face as Dr. Burr felt her abdomen first, then reached inside. Dana knew even before the doctor said the second baby was breech.

"Not to worry. I'll try to turn the little darling," the doctor assured her. "Otherwise, sometimes we can pull him out by his feet. Let's just give it a few minutes. The second baby is generally born about fifteen minutes after the first."

Dana looked over at her son now in the bassinet where a nurse was cleaning him up. "He looks like you," she said to her husband and turned to smile up at him as another contraction hit.

LIZA REACHED THE BACK of the car. She could hear movement inside. "Jordan!" she called. A moment later the back hatch clicked open and began to rise. She stepped to the side, weapon leveled at the darkness inside the SUV, cursing herself for not having her flashlight. "Jordan?"

A moan came from inside, then more movement.

"Liza, he has a gun!" Jordan cried.

The shot buzzed past her ear like a mad hornet. She ducked back, feeling helpless as she heard the struggle in the car and could do little to help. Another shot. A louder moan.

"I'm coming out," Wyatt Iverson called from inside the SUV. "I'm not armed."

"I have him covered," Jordan yelled out. "But you can shoot him if you want to."

Liza leveled her weapon at the gaping dark hole at the back of the SUV. Wyatt Iverson appeared headfirst. He fell out onto the ground. She saw that he was bleeding from a head wound and also from what appeared to be a gunshot to his thigh. She quickly read him his rights as she rolled him over and snapped a pair of handcuffs on him.

"Jordan, are you all right?" she called into the vehicle. She heard movement and felt a well of relief swamp her as he stumbled out through the back. "What is going on?"

"He planned to bury me in this trench," Jordan said. "I think Shelby is in the other car. I suspect he killed her before he put her down here."

Wyatt was heaving, his face buried in his shoulder as he cried.

"Can you watch him for a moment?" Liza asked, seeing that Jordan was holding a handgun—Wyatt's, she assumed.

She holstered her own weapon and climbed up over the top of the SUV to the next one. Dirt covered most of the vehicle except the very back. She wiped some of the dirt from the window and was startled to see a face pressed against the glass.

There was duct tape over Shelby's mouth. Her eyes were huge, her face white as a ghost's. Blood stained the front of her velour sweatshirt where she'd been shot in the chest at what appeared to be close range since the fabric was burned around the entry hole.

Liza pulled out her cell and hit 911. "We'll need an ambulance and the coroner." She gave the dispatcher directions, then climbed back over the top of Jordan's rental SUV to join him again.

Wyatt was still crying. Jordan, she noticed, was more banged up than she'd first realized. He was sitting on the SUV's bumper. He looked pale and was bleeding from a shoulder wound.

"Come on, let's get out of this trench before the sides cave in and kill us all," she said. "Are you sure you're all right?"

He grinned up at her. "Just fine, Deputy," he said, getting to his feet. "I sure was glad to see you."

As she pulled Wyatt to his feet and the three of them staggered up out of the hole, she smelled the pine trees, black against the night sky. The air felt colder as if winter wasn't far behind. She looked toward Lone Peak. The snow on the top gleamed in the darkness. Everything seemed so normal.

The rifle shot took them all by surprise. Wyatt suddenly slumped forward and fell face-first into the dirt. Jordan grabbed her and knocked her to the ground behind one of the huge tires of a dump truck as a second shot thudded into Wyatt's broad back.

Liza rolled and came up with her weapon. She scrambled over to Wyatt, checked for a pulse and finding none, swore as she scrambled back over to Jordan out of the line of fire. She could hear the sound of sirens in the distance. It was too dark to tell where the shot had come from.

But over the high-pitched whine of the sirens, she heard a vehicle start up close by. "Stay here," she ordered Jordan and took off running toward her SUV.

A SECOND SON WAS BORN seventeen minutes after the first. Dana began to cry when she saw him.

"Identical twin boys," Dr. Burr told her. "Congratulations."

Hud hugged her. "We really have to quit doing this," he whispered. "I can't take it."

She laughed through her tears. No one was more fearless than her husband, but she knew what he meant. Her heart had been in her throat, afraid something would go wrong. She couldn't bear the thought of losing her babies.

"You did good," the doctor said, squeezing her hand. "Do you have names picked out yet?"

Dana shook her head and looked to Hud. "I have a couple of ideas though."

He laughed. "I'm sure you do. I'd better call everyone."

"You mean Liza," she said. "You haven't heard from her?"

He checked his phone. "No."

She could tell he was worried.

"Jordan left without telling anyone where he was going, but everyone else is out in the hall waiting for the news."

"Go do whatever it is you have to do, Marshal," she said, smiling. "But let me know when you hear from Liza—and my brother."

He grinned at her. "It's going to be so nice to have you back on your feet."

LIZA REACHED HER PATROL SUV just moments after seeing a set of headlights coming out of the pines in the distance. Jordan was hot on its heels. He leaped into the passenger seat as she started the engine. She hurriedly turned around and went after the killer.

The other vehicle was moving fast. She saw the headlights come around as the vehicle hit the narrow strip of pavement, the driver almost losing control.

Liza followed the other vehicle headed down the mountain. The road was treacherous with lots of switchbacks. She had to assume whoever had killed Wyatt knew the road. But the driver was also running scared.

She glanced over at Jordan. He needed medical attention. "You should have stayed back there to wait for the ambulance," she said as she managed to keep the vehicle in front of her in sight. "Call and tell the ambulance to wait in Meadow Village. The coroner might as well wait, too."

"See, you would have missed my company if I hadn't come along," he said. "And Wyatt wasn't great company when he was alive, let alone dead."

She shot him another look, worried that he might be hurt worse than she thought. "Did he say anything about why he killed Shelby?"

"We didn't get to talk much. He knew she vandalized his father's equipment. I don't think he took it well. He swore he didn't kill Alex. But he killed Tanner and Alex has been blackmailing Wyatt for years, writing it off as a business expense."

Liza suspected that whoever had killed Alex

Winslow had just killed Wyatt Iverson as well, but why? Shelby was dead. So who had just shot Wyatt?

"All of this started because Shelby was going to force Tanner into marriage, one way or the other," Jordan said. "When he broke up with her, she vandalized the construction equipment he was responsible for to get even with him. She hadn't given a damn whose equipment it was. Ironic it turned out to be her future father-in-law's. And look where the repercussions of that one malicious act have landed us all."

The vehicle ahead swung through a tight curve, fishtailed and for a moment Liza thought the driver would lose control and crash. She could make out a figure behind the wheel, but still couldn't tell who it was. All the SUVs looked similar.

Liza knew who wasn't behind the wheel of the car in front of her. Shelby was dead. So was Malcolm Iverson and his son Wyatt. Alex had found the photographs and gotten himself killed when he'd blackmailed Shelby— her husband. She'd been so sure that Wyatt had killed Alex because of it. Alex had somehow figured out that Wyatt had killed Tanner.

Now she suspected that the last piece of the puzzle was in that SUV ahead of her. Whoever had shot Wyatt Iverson must have shot Alex. But why? Was it possible Alex had been blackmailing someone else?

Ahead she caught a glimpse of the lights of Meadow Village. She was right behind the vehicle in front of her. The driver didn't stand a chance of getting away.

She thought about the photos and tried to remember if there was anything else in them. "That one photograph," she said more to herself than to Jordan. "Wasn't it of Tanner and Tessa coming out of the woods?"

"Like I said, Shelby thought of everything."

"Including making her best friend go into the woods with Tanner?"

Jordan let out a curse. "I never could understand why Tessa did what Shelby told her to. She said Shelby even talked her into marrying Danny Spring, when apparently she has always been in love with Alex."

Liza felt a chill race up her spine. "But Alex had these photographs. He would have seen Tessa coming out of the woods with Tanner."

"What are you saying?" Jordan asked.

"Alex would have known just how far Tessa would go to protect Shelby. So why give her the photographs for safekeeping?"

"That's what I said. Unless he *wanted* her to look at the photos. But once she did, why wouldn't she destroy them to protect Shelby?"

"Because she was through protecting Shelby," Liza said. "Shelby had finally done something that she couldn't forgive. Alex's estranged wife believed Alex was having an affair with *Shelby.* I suspect Tessa thought the same thing."

"That would have been the last straw for Tessa. She would have felt betrayed by all of them."

"You're saying if Tessa found out, it would have been the last straw."

Ahead the SUV fishtailed on one of the turns and Liza had to back off to keep from hitting it.

"Tessa. She's in that car, isn't she?" Jordan said. "She used to go out shooting for target practice before hunting season with Shelby and the rest of us. She always pretended to be a worse shot than Shelby, but I always suspected she was better and just didn't dare show it.

She's been hiding her light under a bushel for years, as my mother used to say."

"Not anymore," Liza said as the vehicle ahead of them went off the road on the last tight turn. It crashed down into the trees. Liza stood on the brakes. "Stay here or I'll arrest you!" she shouted to Jordan and jumped out.

With her weapon drawn she hurried to where the SUV had gone off. She hadn't gone far when she heard the shot.

Liza scrambled down into the trees, keeping out of the driver's sights until she finally reached the back of the vehicle. She saw that just as she'd suspected, Tessa was behind the wheel. There was a rifle next to her, the barrel pointed at her. She was bleeding heavily from the crash and the gunshot wound to her side, but she was still breathing.

Liza quickly called for the ambulance. "Just stay still," she told Tessa. "Help is on the way."

Tessa managed a smile. "There is no help for me. Is Wyatt dead?"

"Yes."

"And Shelby?"

"She's dead, too."

Tessa nodded. "Good. They all ruined my life."

"Why kill Alex, though?" Liza asked. "I thought you loved him?"

Tessa got a faraway look in her eyes. "Alex was the only man I ever really loved. I thought he loved me but he was only using me. He said he forgave me for the past, but he lied. He used me just like Shelby and Wyatt used me." She smiled sadly. "They all used me. But I showed them. I wasn't as good at playing their games, but I was always a better shot than any of them."

Epilogue

The hospital room was packed with well-wishers, flowers, balloons and stuffed animals. Dana looked around her and couldn't help the swell of emotion that bubbled up inside of her.

"It's the hormones," she said as she wiped her eyes.

Clay and Stacy had brought Hank and Mary to the hospital to see their new little brothers.

"Hank wants to name them after his horses," Stacy told her. "Mary wanted to name them after her dolls." Stacy looked stronger. Hud had promised her that Virgil would never bother her again. Apparently, there were numerous warrants out on him, including the fact that he'd broken his probation. So added to the latest charges, Virgil would be going back to prison for a very long time.

Dana watched her elderly ranch manager make his way through the crowd to her. Warren Fitzpatrick was as dried out as a stick of jerky and just as tough, but he knew more about cattle than any man she'd ever known. He'd also been there for her from the beginning. As far as she was concerned he was a permanent fixture on the Cardwell Ranch. She'd already promised him a spot in the family cemetery up on the hill.

He gave her a wink. "That's some cute little ones. I just had a peek at them down the hall. Goin' to make some fine ranchhands," he said with a chuckle. "I've got a couple of fine saddles picked out for them. Never too early for a man to have his own saddle."

She smiled up at him. It was the first time she'd ever seen a tear in his eye.

Her father arrived then with a giant teddy bear. "How's my baby girl?" he asked. She'd always been his baby girl—even now that she was the mother of four and only a few years from forty.

"I'm good," she said as she leaned up to hug him. He put the bear down and hugged her tighter than usual.

"I was worried about you," he whispered.

"I'm fine."

"Yes, you are," he said, smiling at her.

Then Uncle Harlan came in with the second giant teddy bear and her father grinned, knowing that she'd thought he'd forgotten she was having twins.

Her father-in-law called. Brick Savage had been sick for some time, but he promised to make the trip down from his cabin outside West Yellowstone to see his new grandsons soon.

"I think we should all leave and let her get some rest," Hilde said to the crowd of friends and family.

"I agree," Hud said. He looked exhausted and so did Liza, who'd stopped in earlier. It had been a shock to hear about the deaths up on the mountain and Tessa Ryerson Spring's involvement. Tessa had died before the ambulance got to her.

Jordan had stopped by earlier, his shoulder bandaged. Dana had hugged him for a long time after hearing what he'd been through. Both he and Liza were lucky to be alive.

Dana noticed that they had left together. She smiled to herself. There was nothing like seeing two people falling in love.

Now as everyone said their goodbyes with Stacy and Clay taking Hank and Mary home, she finally relaxed. Everything was turning out just fine. Stacy had her baby—and a job working for Hilde at Needles and Pins.

"I want to stay around, if that's all right," her sister had said. "I want Ella to know her cousins."

Dana couldn't have been happier. Clay, though, said he would be returning to Hollywood, but that he would come visit more often.

And Jordan, well, Liza was right. Jordan *had* changed. Love did that to a man, she thought, studying her own husband as he came back into the room pushing two bassinets.

"I thought you'd like to see your sons," he said. "Isn't it time you told me what names you've picked out? I know you, Dana. Or do you want me to guess?"

She merely smiled at him.

Hud laughed and shook his head. "You do realize what you're doing to these two innocent little boys by naming them after our fathers, don't you?"

Dana nodded. "I'm giving them a little bit of family history. It isn't just about the ranch. It's about the lives we've carved out here."

Hud looked into the bassinets. "Angus?" he asked as he picked up one of their sons. "And Brick?" He handed her both infants. "So when is the building going to start on the new house?" he asked as he climbed up in the bed beside her and the babies.

"What new house?"

"Jordan's. You know he's staying."

"Did he tell you that?" she asked, unable to keep the hope out of her voice.

Hud gave her a disbelieving look. "You know darned well he is. I wouldn't be surprised if you haven't already picked out a spot on the ranch for him and Liza to live."

"You're taking this pretty well," Dana noted.

He chuckled at that. "Your mother always said Jordan would be back. Stacy, though, I think even that would have surprised your mother."

Dana nodded. "Mom did know her children. She always knew that one day you and I would be together. Mary Justice Cardwell was one smart woman."

"So is her youngest daughter," he said and kissed her.

LIZA REINED IN HER HORSE and looked out over the canyon. The day was warm and dry, possibly one of the last before winter set in. A light breeze stirred the fallen aspen leaves and sighed through the pine boughs.

Jordan brought his horse up beside hers.

"It's beautiful, isn't it?" she said.

"Yes. Beautiful."

She heard something in his voice and looked over at him. He was grinning at her and not looking at the view at all.

"She is *very* beautiful."

"You know you can't charm me," she said, embarrassed. No one had ever told her she was beautiful before. Cute, maybe. Unusual, often. But not beautiful. It wasn't even the word that warmed her to the toes of her boots, though. It was the way he looked at her. He made her *feel* beautiful.

She thought of the scars she'd carried since high school. This case had brought back those awful years, worse, those awful feelings about herself. It had also brought Jordan back to the canyon, a surprise in so many ways.

"You think I'm trying to charm you?" He chuckled as he swung down from his horse.

Before she knew what was happening, he cupped her waist with his large hands and pulled her off her horse and into his arms.

"No, Miss Turner, quite the opposite," he said, his lips just a breath away from hers. "You're the one who's charmed me. All I think about is you. You're like no one I've ever known. I'm under your spell."

She shook her head and laughed softly.

"I'm serious, Liza. You have me thinking crazy thoughts."

"Is that right?"

"Oh, yeah. I've been thinking that I want to stay here and work the ranch with my sister. How crazy is that? Worse, right now, I'm thinking there is only one thing that could make this day more perfect."

She grinned at him. "I'm afraid to ask."

"I'm the one who is afraid to ask." He dropped to one knee. "Marry me and make an honest man out of me."

"Jordan—"

"I know this seems sudden. We should probably at least go on a real date where I'm not just another one of your suspects."

"Be serious."

"I am. I've fallen hopelessly in love with you. Say you at least like me a little." Jordan looked into her wide green eyes and thought he might drown in them. "Just a little?"

"I like you."

He grinned.

"A lot. But marriage?"

"Yes, marriage because I'm not letting you get away, Deputy, and I can't stand to spend another day away from you. I'd marry you right now, but we both know that my sister Dana isn't going to allow it. She's going to insist on a big wedding at the ranch. But that will give us time to go on a few dates. So what do you say?"

Liza's laugh was a joyous sound. "What can I say but yes."

He laughed and swung her up into his arms, spinning them both around. As he set her down, he kissed her, then he drew back to look into her lovely face. Their gazes locked. Electricity arced between them, hotter than any flame.

"I suppose we should wait until our wedding night," he said ruefully.

"Not a chance," Liza said, putting her arms around him. "I can think of no place more wonderful to make love to you the first time than up here on this mountain."

THE WEDDING OF JORDAN CARDWELL and Liza Turner was a glorious affair. Hud and Clay gave Liza away, and stood up with Jordan. Hilde and Dana were Liza's attendants. Hilde had made Liza's dress, a simple white sheath that made her feel like a princess.

The ceremony was short and sweet and held in the large house on the ranch. Stacy baked the wedding cake and the kids helped decorate it. There were balloons and flowers and music. Jordan's father and uncle came with their band to play old-fashioned Country-Western music for the affair.

Neighbors and friends stopped throughout the day to offer felicitations. Even Brick showed up to congratulate them on their wedding and Liza on solving the Tanner Cole case.

The murders and deaths had rocked the small community. Only a few people knew the story behind them and the twisted motives of those involved.

Fall and winter had come and gone. Jordan had been right about Dana insisting on a big wedding. It was spring now. The canyon was turning green from the tall grass on the ranch to the bright leaves on the aspen trees. Work had begun on a ranch house up in the hills from the main house for the two of them.

Liza had never been so happy. She had loved this family even before she fell in love with Jordan. Now she was a part of it. Raised as an orphan, she'd never known this kind of family. Or this kind of love.

Construction on their house on the ranch wasn't quite done, but would be soon. In the meantime, the two of them had been staying in Liza's condo and dating.

Jordan had insisted on a honeymoon. "Hawaii? Tahiti? Mexico? You name it," he'd said.

But Liza didn't want to leave Montana. "Surprise me," she'd said. "Wherever you take me will be perfect."

"How did I get so lucky?" he asked and kissed her as they left in a hail of birdseed.

She had no idea where they were going. She didn't care. With Jordan she knew it would always be an adventure.

* * * * *

REQUEST YOUR FREE BOOKS!
2 FREE NOVELS PLUS 2 FREE GIFTS!

♦Harlequin®
INTRIGUE®
BREATHTAKING ROMANTIC SUSPENSE

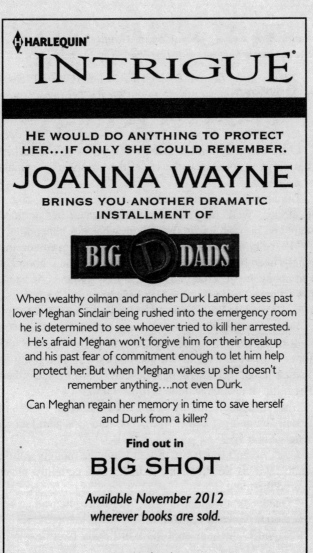

*Something's going on in Conard County's high school…
and Cassie Greaves has just landed in the middle of it.*

Take a sneak peek at RANCHER'S DEADLY RISK
by New York Times *bestselling author Rachel Lee, coming
in November 2012 from Harlequin® Romantic Suspense.*

"There comes a point, Cassie, when you've got to realize
that stuff you got away with as a child is no longer acceptable
or even legal."

Linc paused, realizing he must seem to be going around
in circles. Well, he probably was, between her damned
scent and his own uncertainty about what was happening.

"I'll be honest with you," he said slowly. "I'm wondering
what's been bubbling beneath the surface at the school that
I'm not aware of. That makes me uneasy. On the one hand,
I'm trying to paint it in the best light because I know these
kids. Or thought I did. I don't want to think the worst of any
of them. On the other hand, I guess I shouldn't make too
light of it. There have been three transgressions we know
about with you. Four, if we add James. I'm not going to
dismiss it, but I'm not going to be Chicken Little yet, either.
The mind of a teenage male is impenetrable."

She surprised him by losing her haunted look and
actually laughing. "You're right, it is. And girls aren't much
better at that age."

Girls weren't much better at any age, he thought a little
while later as he drove her home. He'd certainly never
figured them out.

"Thanks for a wonderful time," she said as he walked her
to her door. "I really enjoyed it."

"So did I," he answered more truthfully than he would
have liked. He had to bite his tongue to keep from suggesting

they do it again.

She was still smiling as she said good-night and closed the door.

He walked back to his truck, keys jingling in his hand, and thought about it all, from the bullying to the rat to the evening just past. The thoughts were still rumbling around when he got home.

Something wasn't right. Something. He'd grown up here, gone to school here, been away only during his college years, and now had been teaching for a decade.

His nose was telling him something was wrong. Very wrong. The question was what. And who.

Find out more in RANCHER'S DEADLY RISK
*by Rachel Lee, available November 2012
from Harlequin® Romantic Suspense.*

HARLEQUIN

American ★ Romance®

Discover the magic of Christmas with two
holiday stories of love and forgiveness in

CHRISTMAS IN TEXAS

Christmas Baby Blessings

by TINA LEONARD

Capri Snow isn't happy when she discovers
that the Bridesmaids Creek Christmastown Santa is her
almost-ex-husband and cop, Seagal West. But when danger
strikes, Seagal steps in to protect his wife, no matter the cost.

&

The Christmas Rescue

by REBECCA WINTERS

When Texas Ranger Flynn Patterson saves Andrea Sinclair
and her infant child from her stalker ex-husband, he finds
himself in more danger than just losing his heart.

Bring the magic of Christmas home
this November 2012.

Available wherever books are sold.